THE CARD
PEOPLE

THE CARD PEOPLE

Part I

The Scissors of Fate

by James Sulzer

FUZE
PUBLISHING
Ashland, Oregon

Book design by Ray Rhamey

Cover art by Caleb Kardell

ISBN 978-0-9974956-7-6

Library of Congress Control Number: 2016953264

DEDICATION

for Will, Rob, and Kate

The beauty of science, the power of friendship, the magic of storytelling—

I watched you learn these truths as you grew,

And you taught them to me again, better and stronger—

With love.

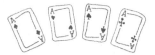

PROLOGUE

Everyone called us the ideal family. Two parents, two kids, always spending time together. Family games of Scrabble after dinner. Dad going for Saturday boat rides with my little brother Sam in the skiff that Sam rowed himself. Dad playing cards with me by the fire before bedtime.

But our family was also a little unusual. For one thing, Mom was blond and fair-skinned, and Dad was from India and had dark skin and hair. Like every family in today's world, both Mom and Dad worked. Mom had a pretty typical job as a guidance counselor at the high school in Bayview, the small town where we live on the north shore of Massachusetts. But Dad worked at MIT, the Massachusetts Institute of Technology, the brainiest place in the world. People called him a genius, and his work was super top-secret.

It was fun and easy being a part of our family. I guess I took it mostly for granted.

The truth is, you never know what you have until you lose it.

It all started with the phone calls late at night. I was used to Dad coming and going at strange hours—he had labs to check on, experiments to oversee, graduate students to direct—but there was something different about these calls. I could hear the tension in his voice. I could feel the worry in his too-quiet footsteps when he took his phone into his bedroom to continue the call. Sometimes I heard a strange car idling outside our house; once I saw a white van sitting there for a couple hours. And one night I came upon Mom in the kitchen, and she was just staring off into space.

Dad had always been busy in his work—in fact, it was amazing he was able to spend so much time with Sam and me, because he put in so many hours at MIT—but he always seemed relaxed and confident. He told me once no man could be happier than he was: he loved his work, and he loved his family.

There came a morning when he was neither relaxed nor confident.

He buzzed into the kitchen looking to grab something to eat for the commute to Cambridge. His favorite breakfast was masala dosa—a type of pancake stuffed with potato and spices.

He sniffed the air disappointedly. "No fresh dosa?"

"Don't you remember? We finished the dosa batter last night, and you didn't get any more from the Indian store," our mom replied. Actually, she sort of snapped at him—which was unusual—but at the same time she flashed a worried look in his direction.

He kept the smile on his face. "Oh yes, I do remember now," he said. Though Dad has lived in the USA for many years, he still has his Indian accent—sort of like a British accent, but more musical.

"Here, darling," Mom said, turning to him and handing him a tall cup. "Take this smoothie." It was the one she made for herself every morning for her breakfast.

"Why, you don't have to do that . . ." Dad began.

"Yes, I do," she replied, giving him a quick kiss.

Dad stopped and looked toward her. An expression came into his dark brown eyes that I'd never seen before, full of pain and sorrow.

And fear.

He opened his mouth to say something, but his eyes filled with tears, and he bent over, gave Sam and me a kiss on the cheek, and fled out the door.

It was the last time we ever saw him.

There are a few different versions of what happened next. I'll give you the official version first.

Early the next evening, I was lying on the couch reading for school. The door shuddered open and Mom staggered in, red-faced and shaking. She was talking on her cell phone and her blond hair was all out of place. She never let that happen to her hair. Her jacket was buttoned wrong. That never happened either.

"You can't know that for sure," she snapped.

"Mom?"

She saw me then. "All right, I'll call again once I get there." She slid her phone into her purse.

"Mom, what's going on?"

"Nothing. A little problem at work," she replied. She yanked out her phone again and glanced at it. "Let's see . . . what's the quickest way to get to Memorial Drive . . ."

"Mom," I retorted, "Memorial Drive is in Cambridge. You don't work there. Dad does." My stomach was churning like a cement mixer.

"Paul, do I have to explain everything I do to you?" Now she was snapping at me—a very unMom-like thing to do. Her blue-gray eyes were gazing past me. "One of the high school kids is there, and she needs help."

I lifted my hands and shook them. "I'm not a little kid. You don't have to hide things from me."

"I'll be back soon," she said. She wouldn't meet my eye.

"Mom, what's going on?" I asked.

She gave me a quick glance. "I love you," she told me. Her eyes glistened, and she was gone.

"Whazzup with Mom?" Sam asked.

Some people say Sam and I look a lot alike, but I think we're as different as can be. I'm tall for my age and skinny, while Sam is as plump as a muffin. What people see is that we both have Dad's coloring, but even there Sam's skin is a little darker than mine. I try hard in school and usually get straight A's; Sam doesn't care about his grades, and he only does his homework when he thinks it's interesting. Which isn't often. And that doesn't play so well with the parental units (as he calls them).

"I don't know," I answered. "She's freaking out about something."

"Why is this family so crazy and uptight recently?" he asked. He took a major bite of his Portuguese toast (the sourdough bread that our town is famous for). He had slathered it with butter and strawberry jam, and he was carrying it around on a ratty old paper towel.

"Something's happened to Dad," I told him.

"How do you know that?" he challenged me.

"I just have this feeling. He's in trouble. Big trouble."

"You're imagining it," he said. "You're always worrying about something." Nothing seems to bother Sam unless he runs out of Portuguese toast and butter. He did a spin move and danced out of the room, followed by Brinda, our beagle, who was drooling big time at the thought of scoring some of his toast and jam.

About an hour later the front door opened and closed, way too quietly. Mom called us into the living room.

"Boys, I have some terrible news," she began, as soon as we were seated on the sofa.

The cement mixer was working overtime in my stomach again.

"What's wrong?" Sam asked.

"Your father has disappeared," Mom said.

"No way," Sam replied.

"What do you mean, *disappeared*?" I asked. "People don't just disappear."

"Well, your father did. He just vanished," she said. Her blue-gray eyes were looking past us. In her early years Mom was an actress in New York and Boston, and for some reason it felt to me now like she was playing a scene.

Sam put his head in his hands. "He's dead," he pronounced slowly. "He's dead and you just don't want to say it." Sam either ignored things completely or else he jumped to the farthest conclusions—there was no middle ground with him.

Mom tried to answer, but the words wouldn't come. She sat down trembling. And then my mom—who never, ever cried—began to sob, with great sighs that shook her whole body.

I turned away my head. A trap door was opening somewhere inside me, and I felt myself tumbling into darkness and horror.

The next thing I knew, I was lying on the sofa, crying—those big wrenching sobs you have when your body feels like you can't even take a breath. Sam was wailing next to me. We had no idea what was happening. All we knew was that our father had disappeared. Whatever that meant. And we were heartbroken.

That was the official story. But there were also the rumors. Sam found out about them first because there's a kid in his fifth grade class, Jeremy Flinks, who's always spreading dirt about people. Half the time it turns out to be nothing, just stuff he made up.

But the other half of the time, it turns out to be true.

Jeremy told Sam that one of his uncles is a policeman in Cambridge. And the uncle was working that night . . .

When there was a car crash. On Memorial Drive.

According to Jeremy, the uncle said it was the strangest thing he'd ever seen. He thought at first it was nothing much, a minor automobile accident. A car had slid off to the side and come to a stop against a guardrail.

This guy, the uncle, was the first policeman to arrive at the scene. He stopped behind the car and approached, flashlight in hand.

He gave a low whistle. For such a minor accident, the damage was extraordinary.

The windows were all broken. The windshield was shattered. The driver was slumped against the steering wheel.

The policeman got a quick look at the man. He had dark skin and seemed to be of Indian descent. He checked the man's pulse. Nothing. There was blood everywhere.

The policeman radioed for help.

Within minutes, the FBI arrived, sent the policeman away, and sealed off the area. The incident disappeared from all official records.

But the policeman had seen something about the man in the car that he would never forget.

The man's upper body and most of his face were punctured in about 100 places by deep, gashing wounds that looked like someone had stabbed him, over and over again, with a super-sharp knife.

1

Sam and I stayed home from school for several weeks, crying a lot, feeling freaked out whenever we passed in front of open windows. Mom was home too—she got the time off from work. We crept around exchanging little unimportant things with each other in muted voices, watching dumb TV shows, and taking a lot of naps.

Sam started to snap out of it before I did. By the end of the third week he said he was bored and wanted to go back to school. I think he missed soccer most of all—he's big into soccer. He's the goalkeeper and he takes it personally if anyone scores off him.

Then on Sam's first day back in fifth grade, Jeremy told him the rumor about Dad. Two days later, Sam decided he'd had enough. He told Mom he couldn't concentrate, he might as well be home. But he kept going to soccer practice, which Mom encouraged him to do.

When I showed no interest at all in returning to school, Mom insisted that I go talk to Mrs. Knockway, the guidance counselor at my middle school where I'm in seventh grade.

"I'm so sorry to hear about your father," she told me. She was a tall woman with very large teeth, which she liked to display in frequent, reassuring smiles. "Would you like to talk about it?"

I tried to, but I couldn't; I just sat there in her office and cried, while she kept handing tissues to me. And it shows how low I felt, that I wasn't even embarrassed to act like that in front of her.

Afterwards, she pulled my mother aside and spoke quietly to her.

"There's no rush, darling," Mom told me later that day. "You'll know when you're ready to go back."

Over the next few weeks, slowly, I began to feel a little different. It was like my legs were coming back under me again. I thought about classmates at school, the wicked funny things some of them said. I remembered conversations with friends over lunch, when we tried to figure out the world.

I realized I felt ready—not just to go back to school—but ready, in some way I can't quite explain, to stand up and fight back. I don't know what was happening exactly. Maybe my love for Dad was starting to get the upper hand over my sadness and fear. By then, Sam was ready too. So finally, a couple months after Dad's disappearance, Sam and I were both back in school, and Mom was back giving out advice to high schoolers.

But things didn't get back to normal. In fact, they only got stranger.

2

One evening after school I was sitting in front of the fire, at the table where Dad and I used to play cards before bedtime. I was surprised to see a deck of cards stacked in the middle, and I noticed something about the Jack of Hearts: it had a bent corner. I remembered that Jack. It was from the last time Dad and I played cards, the night before he disappeared.

Dad was usually all smiles and jokes during our games. His dark brown eyes sort of glowed, and he pushed back his thinning black hair and bent over the table, figuring out his moves.

That night, Mom was in the other room complaining to Sam about another puddle that Brinda had left on the floor. Dad broke open a new deck and took out the cards. He shuffled them once—he always made it look easy even though new cards are pretty stiff and slippery. His hands moved through them like water. Nothing unusual so far.

Then something happened that *was* unusual for him. A card leapt out and fluttered to the floor. A Jack of Hearts.

"I must be losing my touch. Paul, will you pick up that card for me, please?" Something felt a little strange, a little rehearsed, about the way he said it.

"No problem, Dad."

I had to reach awkwardly for the card, and when I picked it up, I bent one of the corners by mistake. I turned to hand it to him and caught him peering out the window. I could tell he was searching for something. When he saw me watching him, he gave a little smile—all's well—but the light in his eyes was dim.

"What game will it be, son?"

"Let's go with high-low Jack."

When Dad was really happy and relaxed, he liked to snack on something sweet. Gulab jamun (fried milk dough flavored with cardamom) was his favorite dessert, but that was reserved for special occasions. Usually he had Marie biscuits with chai tea, which he made himself with fresh ginger and cardamom, pounded together in a mortar and pestle.

He also liked to tell stories as we played. Like about the time he first met Mom, in the bus shelter one wonderful, rainy day, and that chance meeting brought him the greatest happiness in his life, because it led to their marriage and then to us . . . me, then Sam.

But on that last night, Dad wasn't snacking or telling any stories. I was winning tricks one after another, way more easily than usual.

I'd never seen him so distracted. I wracked my brains about how to get him back, and I finally figured it out: Ask him a question about life.

"Dad, what do they mean when they say you have to play the hand that life deals you?" I held up the deck of cards and shook it lightly.

"Oh, that old saying." Dad chuckled, but it wasn't his normal, warm laugh. More like the rattle of bare branches in a January gust. "Well, I suppose it means that we have no power to choose what life gives us. Our strengths, our weaknesses."

I loved his way of talking. It was like a song.

"Do you believe that?" I asked him.

"Oh yes, I do indeed," he answered. He was trying to

sound jolly, but his eyebrows drew together, and his mouth made an unhappy motion, like a little animal wriggling in pain.

"Dad, is something wrong?"

He turned his eyes on me. "Oh no. No, son. It's just that something has occurred to me that I feel I must explain to you. You see, there is one odd thing about life: None of us can really know what our hand is until *after* we've played it."

"Then maybe it doesn't matter how we play it."

He frowned again. "No, ignorance is never an excuse for making a bad decision."

I don't know why I felt like arguing with him then. "But how can we make good decisions if we don't know what we have in our hand?" I asked.

Dad looked suddenly very tired. He spread his cards on the table.

"That's what some of my enemies have been saying for years. But never forget this, Paul: No matter how uncertain life may seem, you can always find your way to an answer. Don't let fear stop you." He turned up the last card. Three Jacks. He had won.

"Enemies?" I blurted out. "Why do you have enemies?"

Dad winced. "I didn't mean 'enemies.' I meant 'rivals.'" He pushed my hair back and gave me a kiss on my forehead.

I knew he meant enemies.

That was the same deck of cards that I held in my hands now. I hadn't seen it for weeks.

I picked up the cards and held them close to my chest, thinking of Dad. That night when I went to bed I brought the cards into my room and placed them on the bedside table.

As I drifted off to sleep I began to wonder: Who had put the deck on the table? Mom? Sam?

And why?

3

I must have just fallen asleep when a tiny voice next to my ear demanded, "Wake up!"

I turned my head in its direction, and I heard it cry, "Stop! Do you want to squish me?" I raised my head and craned it to the side. By the dim glow of the nightlight, I saw a funny little creature with a rectangular body and springy legs—and it was waving its skinny arms and hopping up and down. "Wake up, I say!" Its voice was squeaky and a bit hoarse. "Danger! Distress! Calamities! Wake up!"

I closed my eyes and opened them again. The creature was still there. My eyes hadn't tricked me. It was a little person— no, a card—a living card—a Jack of Hearts, in fact—and it was standing on the bedspread, draped in its fancy royal clothes, peering at me intently. Above the flat card body, its handsome head wore a velvet crown inlaid with rows of tiny pearls.

I blinked again. The card did not go away.

"Are you awake now?" the card asked.

"I'm not sure," I replied.

"Well, decide," it said.

"You're not real, are you?" I asked sleepily.

"Are you?" the card replied, and it reached forward and touched me lightly on the hand.

I flinched, startled. Its touch had about as much force as a grasshopper . . . but still, it *touched* me.

As my knees jerked up under the bedspread, the card flipped up into the air, twirled backwards, and landed on its back at the foot of the bed. I took a breath and leaned forward.

It looked like a normal old card now, nothing more.

I must have been imagining it all. I must have been dreaming.

But then, slowly and with no sign of haste, the card pushed itself back to its feet, removed its little crown, dusted it off, and placed it firmly on its head, then the strange fellow took a step or two across the bedspread towards me.

I screamed and leaped out of bed.

4

I stumbled across the room and slammed sideways into my desk. Some coins clattered onto the floor and rolled about like crazy robots.

"I've lost my mind," I mumbled to myself. I found my way over to the light switch and turned it on.

In the glare of the light the card person was still there. It turned toward me and shook its head mildly.

"You haven't lost your mind," it answered. "But it would help if you would behave more reasonably."

"What *are* you?" I asked.

"It's a long story." The little card put his left foot in front of him and struck a noble pose. "To begin with, I am a Jack, which, as you may know"—here he cleared his throat—"is royalty. But to my friends I am simply Jack."

"Um . . . Jack. Can you give me any reason why I should think you're real?" I asked.

"Didn't the deck of cards join you on the table tonight?" he replied.

"So it did move there," I mumbled.

"We hadn't been fully activated yet, but we had some powers already," Jack said. "We wanted to make you feel better."

"But why?" I asked.

"We don't know," he replied. In some ways he seemed as mystified as I was.

"Things aren't great with me," I admitted. "My father's missing . . . maybe worse than missing." I lowered my head.

Jack's little eyebrows sort of wrinkled. "I see. I'm very sorry."

"Thanks."

"Maybe we can help you. And if I may be so bold, perhaps you might be able to help us." Now that I was more used to it, Jack's voice didn't sound all that squeaky; it was small and delicate, like the whisper of wind through beach grass.

"Help you how?" I asked.

"An enemy wishes to destroy us. We need your help."

That word: *enemy*. I felt a shiver. "Why me?"

"We don't know why, but we like you and we trust you." Jack pulled himself to his full height and raised his tiny chin. The combination of majesty and paper-thin vulnerability went right to my heart.

"I'll help," I said.

"Splendid."

He took a step forward. "You help us against the scissors people, and we will help you find your father."

"That sounds good . . ." I began. Then I did a double take. "Did you say *scissors people*?" I asked.

Jack nodded. "The scissors people. Maybe you'd prefer not to get involved? It might be dangerous." There was an urgent tone in his remark.

"Of course I'll help. I'll do whatever I can."

I stuck out a finger, and Jack climbed up onto it. He felt about as heavy as a cricket or a June bug. "I'd like you to meet Sam, my brother," I said. "Would that be okay?"

"It will be a pleasure," he replied.

As his head, arms and legs slid back into the card, I packed him into the box and creaked open my bedroom door.

5

I glanced down the hall. Sam's light was still on under his door—the poor guy had trouble going to sleep these days. I knocked softly (so as not to wake up Mom) and slipped into his room. The little bro was sitting up in bed, reading one of his zillion adventure novels about soccer. As usual, on his laptop next to him, he had some of his favorite YouTube videos going: the great soul groups of the 1960s—most of them from his favorite group, the Temptations. Brinda was curled up on her dog bed in the corner.

"'Sup?" he asked.

In the soft light of the reading lamp, his face looked a little puffy.

"Hey," I said.

The springs squeaked as I sat down next to him. I glanced around the room. "Are you sure you have enough pictures of soccer players?" The walls were plastered with photos that Sam had torn out of magazines and taped to the walls.

"What do you want?" he asked.

"There's some crazy stuff going on."

Sam put down his soccer book and sat up. "You mean Dad?"

"Something else." I took the deck of cards out of the box, tapped them once or twice, and set them down in a neat pile on the bedside stand. "Don't say anything, just watch," I told him.

"Uh . . . I think I've seen a deck of cards before, Paul."

"Just watch, okay?"

For a minute, nothing happened. Sam moved around a little, scratched his neck, and crossed his arms. He gave me one of his looks. For a little pudge of a guy, he can cop quite an attitude when he wants to.

Finally, just when it seemed like nothing would ever happen, the top card began to tremble slightly, as if a mini-earthquake were erupting beneath it. Sam gave me a quick glance and leaned in closer. The entire deck began to shake and then, with the agility of a grasshopper, Jack slid himself out of the deck, stood up, stretched his arms over his head, extended his head, took a look about the room, and strolled toward us.

"What the heck is going on?" Sam gasped.

"Don't call Mom!" I warned.

Jack drew himself up to his full height. "Is this Master Sam?" he asked me.

"It is," I replied. "Sam, I would like to introduce you to the Jack of Hearts. His friends call him Jack."

Sam gulped. His mouth worked soundlessly open and shut, like a goldfish. His eyes bulged, and he pulled himself back into a corner of the bed.

"A pleasure," Jack said. "A pleasure to meet the brother of our protector." Bending his skinny little legs, he swept his arm and gave a courtly bow.

"Say hello, Sam," I told him.

"Hello, Sam," Sam murmured, his eyes still bulging.

Jack sniffed the air. "He's your blood brother. Same DNA."

"How can you tell that?" I asked.

"The smell. It's the same as the DNA in the teardrops that brought us to life."

Teardrops that brought them to life? What was he talking about?

Jack turned toward Sam. "Please don't be alarmed, little brother. It is important for you to understand that this is only the first of many unusual, possibly unpleasant events in your world—until we find success."

"What is he saying, Paul?" Sam asked quietly. "Is he threatening us?"

"No. He's a card person," I told him. As if that explained anything.

"How'd he get here?"

"I don't know. How'd we get here?" I asked back.

"Is he going to hurt us?"

"No. He and the rest of the deck are on our side."

Sam glanced nervously at the deck. "What do they want?"

Jack took a step forward. "Master Sam, we wish to request your help . . . with the scissors people."

"Scissors people?" Sam asked. At this point, I think he officially entered information overload.

Jack glanced back and forth between us. "We're expecting an attack late tonight," he confided, "and we're hoping you can help. But first, would you care to meet the others?"

Sam looked at me and gave an eyebrow shrug.

"We'd love to," I told Jack.

"Then let's return to our base of operations—that is, to your room," he said.

Sam looked Jack up and down, smiled, and offered his finger.

6

Back in my room, Jack gave a command, and the other cards began to wake up. Soon they had spread out on my desk in various stages of sitting, standing, stretching . . . fifty-two little people in four families. The number cards were the children, and the smaller the number, the younger the card. The Twos and Threes were just learning to walk, and they stumbled about on their short, stubby legs, bumping into each other and cooing. Some of the Fours and Fives were racing around playing tag and chirping like little peepers.

The older cards, with their longer legs, were playing a game of running and broad jumping (except that the jump was more like a long glide), and some of the younger cards were trying to copy them. The Four of Clubs fell down and started crying, and the Nine picked her up and soothed her, stroking her little clover-shaped face and telling her everything would all right.

Sam gave me a pleased look.

The bodies of the card people looked like normal cards—the Four of Spades had a spade in each corner of her body, and the number "4" in the top left corner. The Three of Diamonds had three diamonds down the middle of his body, like buttons on a shirt.

The heads were connected to the bodies by thin, flexible necks. The younger ones' faces were flat, but the Jacks, Queens and Kings (like the Jack of Hearts) had human faces and roundish, 3-D heads. The face cards wore fancy jackets and robes over their card bodies.

The Aces had A-shaped faces and triangular hands and feet and glided through the air silently. Each one seemed to be in its own orbit.

The door pushed open, and Brinda clambered into my room and stood on the rug, her tail wagging. She gazed curiously toward the card people, then trotted over for a sniff. The children took turns running up to her, being tickled by her nose, and falling back on the desktop in gales of giggles.

"That giant creature stinks to high heaven!" the Eight of Diamonds exclaimed. He took a step toward Brinda, sniffed loudly, staggered off, and pretended to faint.

"He's right about that," Sam commented to me. "Did you know, beagles hold down third place on the list of the world's stinkiest dogs?" My brother is proud of his knowledge of trivia.

Meanwhile, Jack and some of the Kings and Queens stood off to one side, pointing at Brinda and talking. They seemed to be finalizing their plan.

A few minutes later the Queen of Spades cleared her throat, and the cards froze.

"Places, everyone. Gather on the Common."

In silence, the cards sorted themselves into four lines, ran straight down the four legs of the desk, and swarmed up the side of my bed and onto the bedspread. They were in perfect formation: four lines determined by suit and rank, from King down to Two. Some of the children were pushing and shoving, but after a bit of scolding from their elders, they stopped. The Aces stood off to one side, together, like a quartet of vultures.

The cards had at first lined up facing away but now, at a word from the King of Spades, they turned in unison, shimmering like a flock of birds. Now every card faced Sam and me.

The King of Spades took a step forward and looked up at me. His nose was wrinkling.

"Are you the human?" he asked.

"Yes," I replied. "And this is a human also." I nodded toward Sam, who stood up very straight and tall.

"I told you he was," the Queen of Spades muttered.

"Yes, dear, but I wanted to be sure," the King replied. "Very well. I would like to explain to you what the Aces have reported to us."

"I'm all ears," I said.

The King took another step forward and peered up at me. He looked puzzled. "You're not *all* ears. I see only two," he replied. "Though they *are* quite large."

"That's just an expression, dear," the Queen replied.

"Very well," the King said, nodding his head sagely. "Well, in short, here is our predicament." He cleared his throat. "A group of evil beings are planning an attack on our people tonight. They have taken on the shape of something especially deadly to us—two sharpened, inclined planes affixed in the middle."

"Scissors," Jack explained. "The scissors people."

"Yes, that's their name," the King agreed. "According to our intelligence, the scissors people are gathering in their base on the far shore of the bay, where they first sprang to life. They are preparing to cross the bay shortly before dawn and make their attack while the humans sleep."

"Not that anyone, even a human, could fight off such a deadly assault," the Queen added.

"Will you be willing to help us?" the King asked.

Sam and I exchanged a glance. "How hard could it be, Paul?" he whispered.

"I know," I whispered back. I think we were both picturing those little scissors that kindergartners use, with rounded edges and plastic handles.

Sam tapped me on the shoulder. "I mean, if we arm ourselves with cookie sheets . . ."

"Yeah, or pots or pans."

We nodded at each other.

"Of course we'll help," I told the King. "Tell us what we can do."

He explained the plan, which—we soon learned—had nothing at all to do with pots, pans, or cookie sheets.

"Our plan involves that creature!" he declared, pointing toward Brinda, who stood up, walked over to the King, and allowed him to pet her black, dimpled nose.

7

"By any chance, do you have another deck of cards?" Jack asked me.

I opened a drawer in my desk, found an old deck, and placed it on the bed: *Ta-ta*.

The Ten of Clubs began picking up the cards and handing them out, one by one. "Seven of Diamonds!" he called, and the Seven of Diamonds (the card person) marched over and took his matching card. The rest of the card people followed suit, setting their appropriate cards on the bed face up, then patting down every square centimeter of them with their tiny hands.

"What the heck!" Sam exclaimed. "It's like fifty-two massages going on all at once!' he exclaimed. It was the first time I'd seen Sam smile in a long time.

When the process was completed, the card people piled the old deck on the floor in the center of the room. Then Jack hopped back onto my shoulder.

"Those are our decoys," he told me.

"I think I get it!" I replied.

Jack asked for some string, which I found in another drawer in my desk. "Now, if you would pack us back into our box, and then tie us beneath the stomach of your charming beast . . ." he said, pointing toward Brinda. She sniffed at him and began to lick him with her red tongue. He turned his head away and exclaimed, "Oh stop that, will you, darling? It tickles!" She stopped and he petted her on the snout. "Once we're tied in place, kindly let Brinda outside . . . and we will be on our way," he told me.

"Are you ever coming back?" Sam asked. He seemed worried that we might lose the card people too.

"Oh yes, we'll be back at daybreak. It will be safe for us here by then. As for you . . ." he began.

"Yeah, what about *us*?" Sam asked. "What's gonna keep *us* safe?"

Jack nodded. "To the best of our knowledge, the scissors people have no knowledge of you or interest in harming you—not yet anyway. But you would do well to hide in there for the rest of the night." He pointed toward my closet.

"Okay. Anything else?" I asked.

"Well," he replied, "in order to avoid detection, it wouldn't hurt to mask your odor. The scissors people use their highly advanced sense of smell to locate their victims. Do you have something you might put on your skin to hide its scent?"

"Deodorant!" Sam replied. "I've been telling you for weeks, you need to start using it, Paul." He waved his hand in front of his nose.

I ignored him. "A lot of foods have a strong smell," I suggested.

"Mom's coffee?" Sam asked.

"That wouldn't stick to us," I replied. "How about some of Mom's stinky cheese?"

"Oh, yeah, that Epoisses stuff! That's totally rank!" Sam exclaimed.

Jack was listening with interest. "Would you get a sample so that I might smell it?"

I crept downstairs to the kitchen, pulled open the refrigerator quiet as a cat, and brought back one of Mom's wheels of Epoisses. She was crazy about the stuff. I opened the top, and

Jack stuck his head down in the container and quickly drew back.

"That will do the job!" he exclaimed. "Smear it on any exposed skin you have, and you will definitely escape detection."

Sam never needed any encouragement to do something gross. He dipped his hand down into the container and began to spread the white, drippy stuff over his face and neck. After a minute he looked like a very strange ghost—a ghost who was melting and dripping—and he smelled like a dead animal. "Let's hope Mom doesn't think we're crackers . . . she might find us and eat us," Sam added. It was the first joke I'd heard him make in a long time. Not that it was a good joke. But by the way he chortled, I guess he found it amusing. And it was good to hear a little laughter coming back into our lives after all these months.

But he knew as well as I did that this wasn't all fun and games. The scissors people would be here soon, and if he was anything like me, he was getting a feeling in the pit of his stomach like a lead cannon ball.

8

A few minutes later we brought Brinda downstairs and propped open the back door, and she disappeared outside with her cargo of card people. Back in my room, I smeared myself with cheese. Sam and I slipped into the closet, with the door open just wide enough for us to watch.

The old deck of cards lay on the floor in the middle of the room.

The minutes stretched into an hour, then two hours.

"I don't think they're coming," Sam declared. He yawned and snuggled down next to me. He pulled a sweatshirt over himself. His eyes fluttered shut. "Wake me if anything happens." Soon he was snoring like a mole.

The stench of the cheese was pretty bad at first, but after awhile you didn't notice it so much. I wondered if there are other unpleasant things that we grow accustomed to, without knowing it . . .

Not much later I drifted off to sleep, blinked awake for a minute, and drifted off again, then woke up again. Somehow I could tell it was getting very late.

Finally, a sound woke me once and for all. A sinister clank.

I sat up and peered out through the crack in the door. I elbowed Sam, who sat up beside me.

Three pairs of scissors stood in the doorway. They began to move across the floor, with twisting, stiff-legged motions which glinted in the dim nightlight. They were about six inches tall, with silver blades and black handles. These were no kindergartner's scissors. The points looked as sharp as samurai swords. Small, dark, expressionless eyes hung suspended in the middle of the handles.

To me, the eyes were the scariest thing of all—their blank cruelty.

More scissors followed in their wake, lurching from side to side like zombies. They moved in unison—left, right, left, right—and the sound of their points clacking on the floor echoed through the room like distant gunfire.

They were no more than a few yards from the center of the room when they stopped. The eyes began to rove about—taking in all the corners of the room. I wasn't sure if they saw us. With weird clinking sounds, they leaned toward one another.

"I'm scared, Paul," Sam whispered in my ear.

"Shhh!" I told him. My stomach felt like it was free-falling from an airplane.

Like lines of enchanted toy soldiers, the scissors pressed forward. Just a few feet of bare wood floor separated them now from the cards.

"Paul, look at the ones in the back!" Sam called softly.

Three of the scissors in the back line had floated up into the air and rotated ninety degrees so that their pointed ends were facing forward. They hung there like small missiles, ready to launch. They were followed by more rows of three scissors each, hanging in the air.

The foot soldiers marched up to the deck of cards and leaned over it together, each one shaking slightly, like an animal drawing in repeated breaths. Again they leaned in toward one another and touched blades. They turned to the hovering scissors, nodded, and stepped to either side.

The airborne scissors hurtled forward in one mad rush. You could feel the whiff of air as they streaked past us.

They struck the deck of cards with savage intensity, sending the cards flying in all directions. They pursued them about the room, snapping like demented alligators.

Sam gripped my arm, squeezing so tight that it hurt.

Bits of cards, all sizes and shapes, filled the air, and the scissors chased them down like sharks feeding on a school of defenseless fish.

In less than a minute, it was done. The floor was littered with little pieces of plastic, white, black, and red. The scissors were now hovering in the air near each other, forty or fifty of them in all. They touched blades again—it seemed to be their way of communicating—and formed a circle. The circle began to revolve, slowly and triumphantly. It wheeled around another minute or two, as if in a victory dance, and then the individual scissors peeled off from the circle and shot out the window, shredding the screen to nothing.

And they were gone.

Beside me, Sam was sobbing. "Horrible . . . horrible . . . Paul, it's horrible!"

Like a monster escaping from a cave, the terror and sadness of the night Dad disappeared had come flooding back over us, made more devastating by the rumor of how his body had been found. I put my arm around Sam and we both cried, our cheesy faces sticking to each other, our tears running down our cheeks in little streams of hopeless sorrow.

9

The next thing I knew, I heard the musical tinkling of little voices outside the closet door.

The card people were back, strolling about the floor of my room and examining the shattered pieces of cards. Brinda lay near them, resting her head on her front paws.

I pushed open the closet door. Jack saw us and hurried over.

"Are you all right?" he asked.

"Yes," I said.

"No," Sam said.

Jack looked up, puzzled. "It was bad," I explained.

"Crazy scary," Sam muttered.

Jack's little eyebrows wiggled. "The scissors people can be quite terrifying, and we will need to devise some sort of a plan to immobilize them. The Clubs are searching for ideas, and we're open to suggestions."

Sam blinked. "Did Brinda protect you last night?" he asked. "I mean, did she smell so bad, they couldn't find you?"

Jack nodded. "Strong odor. Mission accomplished." He winked. "But tell me, how bad was the attack?"

Sam shuddered. "Pure liquid terror," he said.

As Jack listened in silence, a worried look on his face, I described what happened. He asked if the scissors had detected us, and I said I didn't think so.

"Were they really fooled? Did they really think that old deck of cards was you guys?" I asked.

"We believe so," Jack replied. "We transferred as much of our smell to them as is humanly—or cardly—possible."

"So that's why you were patting them like that!" Sam exclaimed. Sometimes my brother is a little slow with these things.

Jack nodded.

Brinda had gotten up and was walking around the room now, sniffing at the bits of cards. She squatted down in one corner.

"No, Brinda!" I called.

Too late. She let go a thunderous stream of pee, right on the wood floor.

"Mom says we're going to have to get rid of her if she keeps doing this," Sam moaned.

"I'll clean it up," I said. I sneaked out into the kitchen and got some paper towels. Meanwhile Sam found the card people some Q-tips, and they bent the ends and used them as push brooms, sweeping the pieces of plastic into a pile to one side of the room.

Just then, as if on cue, our mother called from her bedroom. "Boys? Boys?"

"Yes?" we called back.

"Is everything okay?"

"Everything's fine."

"I thought I heard Brinda barking last night. I don't want her peeing on the floor."

"Don't worry, that won't happen," I replied.

"I'm taking her out for a walk!" Sam called to Mom.

"Wash your face first!" I warned Sam. What was left of the cheese had crusted on his cheeks and forehead like centuries-old cakes of dirt.

I put the card people back in their box, washed my face, and returned to the room to start cleaning. By the time Mom entered the room to check in on me, yawning and still in her nightgown, the last of the evidence was gone. I had even straightened up my desk and picked up my dirty clothes. She smiled when she saw how neat the room was.

"All righty then. Time for breakfast." She started to leave but turned back. "Oh, one more thing."

"Yes?"

"Look at me, please, not at your hands."

I raised my head and met her eyes.

"I've been doing some thinking," she said. "Can you and I sit down and have a talk—in a few days, maybe this weekend?"

"Sure, Mom."

Had she finally decided to tell me the truth about Dad? Could the scissors people have had something to do with it? I was afraid to know.

After breakfast, as I checked my emails, something happened to make the fear worse. There was an unfamiliar email in my Inbox. It had no return address—just the title Samir. The message was only two lines long:

Your father tried to rewrite the laws of creation.

His enemies rejoice at the news of his desolation.

It was signed *HOBO.*

A chill went up my spine. Who or what was HOBO? How did it know about Dad? Was it trying to be helpful . . . or was it laughing at our misery?

But there was no time now to investigate. After a long night, I now had to get through a day of school.

10

I was just short of the path through the woods when I heard a roaring sound. I whirled around to see pickup truck racing down our street, bouncing out of control like a ping-pong ball. What was wrong with adults these days? I crouched behind a tree until the truck was well past, and then I followed the secret path the rest of the way to school.

This route would allow Jack to have his first walk in the woods. I took him out of the box and leaned him up against a rock. He quickly unfolded himself and began to stroll around, quite cheery as always. He scurried after me, chattering happily about the types of grass and the trees and vines. It was April, and the bushes were just starting to green up. Little sticky buds were unfolding in the sunlight.

He stopped just once, when he encountered a beetle that had fallen over on its back and was waving its legs. He pushed the beetle onto its feet again, and hopped back as the beetle gave him one look and ran for its life into the underbrush. A few minutes later, when we came to the end of the path, I picked Jack up again.

For a minute, I actually forgot my worries about Dad.

The middle school in our little town of Bayview, Massachusetts was a two-story, shingled structure that had been designed and built a long time ago. It was small, the teachers were pretty good, and most of the students seemed happy enough.

Not me.

Over the past year, everything had gone wrong. It was like one day our class was one big, happy family, then the next it split into cliques. The girls' cliques were too complicated to try to understand. The boys' were simpler, but just as rigid. There were the athletes, the brains, the tough kids, the misfits . . . and I didn't really fit anywhere, not even with the misfits. Which is sort of funny when you think about it.

For some reason, this year I'd started worrying about what other kids thought of me, which made me a whole lot quieter. Some days it was like a mist of shyness surrounded me.

In the past there was always Nim—my friend since second grade, when she moved to Bayview from Thailand. Back then, she was a small, scared, bright-eyed girl with jet black hair and toothpick arms and legs. Right from the start, even before she could speak a word of English, I knew she'd be my friend. My dad had sometimes talked about how difficult it was for him to get used to America after growing up in India, and maybe that was the reason I wanted to help this new girl.

I taught her some American things—how to play checkers and Connect Four, how to say the names of stuff in the class-room, like chalkboard and reading corner, how to eat American food like hamburgers. (The first time she had a burger, it was pretty funny watching her try to pick it up with a pair of chopsticks.) She shared with me the Thai food she brought from home, and I shared samosas and other Indian foods with her. She quickly learned English, and pretty soon everyone realized she was an amazing student, probably the smartest kid in the entire class. Over the years we had play dates and went bowling and even had some sleepovers. She was a girl, but that never seemed to get in the way.

But now, she'd sprouted up four or five inches—she was almost as tall as me—and begun to dress differently. Sam said to me one night, "Nim used to look like a pencil. Now she looks like a bowling pin. I liked her more as a pencil." And she had been adopted into a new group: the fastest, coolest seventh-grade girls—the in-your-face pretty ones who wore serious makeup and read fashion magazines and were starting to go out on dates with the eighth graders and even with some high school boys.

This morning was typical. When I saw Nim in the hall, she looked away, made a point of talking to her new BFF Kelly, and scissored right past me in her stone-washed jeggings.

"Hey, Nim!" I called after her.

She stopped. Kelly gave her a little look, like are you really going to talk to *that* thing?

"What's up, Paul?" Nim asked. Her gaze was cool.

"Um . . . I have this deck of cards I want to show you."

Sometimes the real Nim still showed through. Her round face broke into a smile. "Oh yeah! Remember when we used to play Spit and—"

"A real deck of cards?" Kelly interrupted, rolling her eyes. "Like with Aces, and Twos, and everything?"

"Yeah . . . it's . . . it's pretty cool," I said.

Kelly took Nim's arm and pulled her away.

"I can't look now. Have fun with it though," Nim called back to me, sort of kind and sort of sarcastic at the same time. She and Kelly swished off, tossing their heads and talking.

For most of the past year I'd kept away from Nim—I didn't want to risk finding out that she really didn't like me anymore. But after all Sam and I had been through, after those months of misery, after finally getting my legs under me again, I wasn't going to hold back any longer. What was there to be afraid of?

I'd try again with Nim in math class, where we had assigned seats next to each other.

11

The problem was Butch and Ken were also in that class.

Our pre-algebra teacher Mr. Ellsbury was a tough grader—so tough that a number of eighth graders were repeating the class from last year. Butch and Ken were the two worst repeaters, and before class each day, they'd pick on one of the seventh grade boys.

Today, as soon as they saw me, they steered right over to my desk, circling like wolves.

"What's that bump?" Ken said, flicking his hand at my chest, where I was carrying the deck of cards. Ken was tall and dark-haired. From a distance he almost looked pleasant. But up close, his eyes had the dull, mean look of a shark.

"Nothing," I replied.

"Little Paulie is developing," Ken and Butch chanted. "Little Paulie is becoming a young woman."

My mouth got as dry as a cornflake. "You guys are really stupid," I told them.

Beside me, Nim took her seat silently. She was glancing away, trying to pretend she didn't see what was happening.

"I wouldn't sit near him if I were you," Butch told her. He was short and blond and built like a fire hydrant.

"Yeah," Ken agreed. "He's got this strange bump growing on him." He flicked his fingers at me.

"What are you guys talking about?" asked a syrupy, I'm-interested voice from across the room. It was Kelly—pretty and red-haired and really stuck on herself.

"We're talking about this weirdo here," Butch told her. "With his weird foods." He waved a hand in front of his nose.

Her pretty brow wrinkled in disgust.

"Maybe we can knock some sense into him," Ken suggested.

"It's worth a try," Butch agreed.

And so they began to smack me on the shoulder and neck with the back of their hands. Nim stood up, but across the way, Kelly signaled to her to stay out of it.

I swatted their hands away. "Leave me alone, you morons!" I said, in my steeliest voice.

No one—not a single person in the class—was lifting a finger to help. So much for the training our school had given us about how to be a responsible bystander.

"Paul's the moron!" the two guys called in soft, jeering voices. "Pervert Paul!"

At that moment, Nim turned to them. There was a look in her eyes that I hadn't seen in a long time.

"That's enough. Leave him alone," she said quietly. Kelly gazed at her in astonishment and shook her head no.

Ken grabbed me from behind, and Butch started to grope me. He found the deck of cards and pulled them out of my pocket.

"Give those back!" I yelled. Butch held the deck of cards off to one side, beyond my grasp, as Ken tightened his hold on me.

I struggled and elbowed and shook and squirmed enough to get my left arm free. With all the force I had, I jammed the heel of my hand against Ken's nose. He grunted and pulled back and I was free.

I dove at Butch. We slammed into the wall and rolled around on the linoleum floor. He jabbed his elbow into my nose, and I felt blood start to pour out.

"What is going on in here?" a man's voice demanded.

Butch relaxed for a moment, and I reached over and smashed him across the chin. The deck of cards fell from his hands, and I snatched them up and jumped back to my feet. The whole front of my shirt and pants were splattered with blood, and blood was still pouring out.

"Paul Kapadia, you are to report to the office immediately," the teacher ordered.

"They started it!" I protested. "They took my cards!"

"I saw you punch him in the face!" Mr. Ellsbury replied sternly. "Go to the office."

"They're the ones you should send to the office!" I argued.

I looked over at Nim, and our eyes met and held.

Nim shook her hair out behind her. From across the room, Kelly was watching her closely.

Nim cleared her throat and took a step forward.

"Ken and Butch started it," she announced. "I saw it all, Mr. Ellsbury. Paul's telling the truth. They were harassing him. They were the ones who attacked him. And they took his cards too." She pulled her shirt down over her bare midriff.

The eighth graders glared at her. Kelly turned away in disgust.

The assistant principal stood in the doorway.

"You three, come with me," he ordered Ken, Butch, and me. After another word to him from Mr. Ellsbury, he added to Nim, "And you too." He grabbed a wad of tissues and handed them to me. "And for God's sake, pinch your nose shut so you don't drip blood all the way down the hall."

"Busted . . ." someone behind us murmured in an admiring tone.

12

Nim and I walked home from school together, in silence most of the way. At ground level everything still looked brown and drab, but spring had brought some touches of green to the maple branches above us. Bright red cardinals hopped about in the treetops, singing back and forth. *Whee whee whee.* In the distance, light shimmered on the waves out in the harbor.

"What happened in math class?" she asked.

I thought, *You turned back into your true self.* But out loud, I said, "I know, those guys were out of their minds, weren't they?"

Her eyebrows pinched. "I felt bad for you. They'll pick on anyone who's different in any way."

"No worries," I said. "I don't care."

"Don't lie to me." She flipped the back of her hand against my shoulder.

It didn't really hurt, but it took me by surprise and I was startled. She quickly added, "It was only a friendly tap."

In the old days we used to joke around like that all the time. We fell into silence again.

"Well, you could have it worse," she observed a few minutes later. "Indoor suspension for two days. At least you don't have an out-of-school suspension like Ken and Butch."

"Yeah."

She took a deep breath. "Paul, I'm really sorry about your dad. I know the whole town is sort of stunned about it. I mean, to just disappear like that . . ."

"Thanks," I said. It was the first time Nim had mentioned Dad.

She chewed on her bottom lip. "Do you have any clues? I mean, I've heard a rumor . . ."

I shrugged. "I don't know whether to believe it or not. No one seems to know anything. But you know how top-secret my Dad's research was."

"What's it called? Nano . . . something."

"Nanotechnology."

She stopped and put her hand on my arm. "Paul, I want to help if I can." She turned so we faced right toward each other.

"Thanks," I said. "Oh . . . and Nim . . . I should warn you. You're in for a little surprise."

"A surprise? Sweet!" She almost sounded herself again, like in the old days. Her amber eyes gazed right into mine, so strong and pretty, I had to blink and look away.

There was a little puddle on our kitchen floor, and I cleaned it up fast. "No need for Mom to see this," I told Nim. "Brinda knows she's in trouble. Notice she didn't come bounding out to greet us."

"Maybe she's with Sam," she replied.

"No, he's at soccer practice."

We took off our shoes (Nim knew that's what we do in my house) and climbed up the stairs to my room. I closed the door and took out the cards and set them on the bedside table.

"Jack, you can bring your friends out now if you want," I whispered.

Nim had stopped by the mirror on my bureau and was looking at the photographs that I'd taped up. Some were of the two of us when we were younger. Making faces inside a photo booth at a carnival. Wearing pajamas, perched on top of a pile of pillows from the sofa.

Then it began.

Jack stood up on the table and stretched his skinny arms over his head. And the other cards stood up and stirred about. The children started playing their jumping and gliding games on the bed.

There was a cry of surprise, and Nim was there beside me.

"OMG. What are they?" she asked. Her mouth had fallen open in shock; her eyes were round and wide.

"They're card people," I explained.

"Where'd they come from?"

"Good question." I told her about finding Jack next to my pillow the night before, I told her about the "scissors people" and how we were able to trick them with the old deck of cards. I told her how Jack helped a bug that morning in the woods.

"Paul," she whispered. "This is amazing and crazy beyond belief!"

"I know. But look, Nim . . . Nobody else knows about them except Sam. Promise me you'll keep the secret."

She nodded. "You have my word."

13

At this point I introduced Nim formally to the cards, and they acknowledged her politely with little bows. The Jack of Diamonds stepped forward on the bed, drew off his crown, and bowed deeply to her. "A pleasure to make your acquaintance, miss," he said.

She curtsied back. "The pleasure is all mine. I'm thrilled to meet you all! I . . . I've never known any card people before." She had regained her poise, and her bright eyes sparkled with excitement, though her mouth still kept flying open from time to time.

"They say we diamonds are rather well appointed—deep pockets, don't you know," the Diamond Jack told her. His large, dreamy eyes gazed steadily into hers. "I hope you wouldn't think it indelicate of me to remark that we treat our ladies well."

"Not at all," Nim replied. "And I think the robe you are wearing is awesome."

Rather hastily, my Jack of Hearts stepped forward and cleared his throat. "Are we done?" he asked.

"Quite done," the Jack of Diamonds replied. Bowing and scraping, he backed majestically away.

Jack shrugged. "Please forgive that intrusion. We're still sorting out some things," he told her.

Nim reached over and touched Jack lightly on the top of his head. "Can you tell me more about yourselves?" she asked.

He allowed her to stroke his face. "What would you like to know?"

Nim was leaning very close to him. "Well, to start with," she asked, "where did you come from? Like, are you people from long ago who came back to life as cards?"

"We're not really sure . . ." he said.

Nim's question reminded me of something that Dad had asked me a few months earlier. *If you could come back in life as anything in the world, what would you choose?* I replied something like, "I don't know. Maybe a Giant Sequoia." Then Dad asked, "Wouldn't you like to know how I would answer that question?"

"Sure," I said. "How would you like to come back to life?"

"As a plum," he said.

"As a plum?" I asked. I wasn't sure I'd heard him right.

"As a plum," Dad repeated, smiling and giving me a look that said, don't forget this.

"Why?" I asked.

"Some day you'll understand," he told me.

At the time, I didn't believe for a second that anything would ever happen to my father.

"We've begun to understand some things about ourselves," Jack told Nim, turning his head so she could stroke the other side. "We know how the card families differ from one another. Spades are brainy and philosophical, Hearts like me are friendly and decisive, Diamonds are stylish and clever, Clubs are humble and good with their hands."

He nodded toward the Aces. "No need for me to mention the special powers of the Aces to fly about and to do surveillance. No matter what our suit, we all seem to have the same impulse to help living things in trouble. We rejoice in the high spirits and goodness of our children."

"Where do you all sleep?" she asked.

"In our box," Jack replied.

"In the box?" Nim asked, giving me a look. "Isn't it cramped in there?"

"We don't mind it," Jack added. "It's for safety reasons."

"You should have a little home. Some place that's more comfortable." She asked me if I had an old shoebox, and I rummaged around in my closet and pulled out a couple of boxes. Nim sat on the floor, took the tops off the boxes, and turned them in her hands, looking them over.

"Do you have a pair of scissors?" she asked me.

At the sound of that word, Jack took a few steps back in horror. He was trembling like a leaf.

"Maybe that's not a good idea," I observed.

Nim's hand flew to her mouth. "Oh . . . I'm so sorry!" she exclaimed.

Jack readjusted his crown and took a step forward. "Not to worry. You are a friend—we can trust you. Please proceed with the scissors."

"You're sure?" Nim asked, and Jack nodded.

I found a pair for Nim, and slowly, carefully she started to cut out various shapes.

The play of the children stopped immediately. They backed away and huddled together near the wall, glancing from time to time at the blades as they sliced through the cardboard.

14

As Nim worked, she and Jack chatted. Somehow they started to discuss the moment when the card people first realized that they were alive.

"The Spades have done the most thinking about all this, and they seem convinced that both we and the scissors people are the product of nanotechnology," Jack said.

"Can you tell me again what nanotechnology is?" Nim asked, turning to me. I told her what I knew. Scientists had been working on ways to create incredibly tiny computers, each no bigger than a hydrogen atom, and then link them together to create amazing new systems of artificial intelligence.

"Didn't your father work on nanotechnology?" Nim asked.

"Yeah. That's how I know a little about it. But I didn't think it was real—not yet anyway."

Jack waited for us to finish. "The Spades are also convinced that we were triggered to our full power by a DNA switch. Or lock, if you prefer," he said.

Now it was my turn to ask for an explanation.

"It seems our creator found a way to ensure that our 'nanimation' wouldn't be activated until it fell into the proper hands—until the correct DNA match appeared."

"You mean until someone trusted and true came on the scene?" Nim asked.

"Exactly," Jack replied. He ran up my leg and climbed up onto my shoulder.

"As far as we can remember," Jack went on, "our first moment of true consciousness was accompanied by the sound of a human crying. In fact, we ourselves were rather damp and salty. It seems that some rather large teardrops had fallen on us."

He tapped me on the cheek.

"I get it," Nim said. "Paul, you were holding the cards, and you were crying. And the DNA in your tears touched the cards: Bingo! So that means . . ."

"It was Dad," I whispered. "Of course. I should have known all along." At some point Dad and I had talked about this very idea. In his easy, casual way, he had mentioned that sometime in the future, everything in the room might be conscious. In theory, he said, millions of tiny computers could be implanted in a grain of dust and dropped onto something inanimate like a paper clip—and the paper clip would then be able to talk and even move about. You could ask it to hold two pieces of paper together or you could tell it to untangle itself from the other paper clips in the drawer. You could tell it to bend itself into a human figure.

"Was it your father?" Jack asked, looking intently toward me. "Did your father make all this happen?"

"It must have been him."

The timing *had* to be more than just coincidence. My father leaves, a few months later the cards arrive . . . almost like that was the plan. But why?

"There's just one thing I don't get about this," Nim said.

"Only one?" I asked.

"Tears are basically salt water. Water and salt both cause things to rust and corrode—we learned that in science, remember? So wouldn't your tears have been bad for the cards—or for anything that's high-tech? Think what happens to a phone if you drop it in the harbor."

Jack nodded. "I believe the tears might have harmed us, if we hadn't dried ourselves on a napkin." He gave me a quick glance. "You know what, Paul? Your friend Nim has just given me an idea!"

But there was no time for him to tell us what it was. Outside in the hallway, muffled voices were moving quickly closer.

"Everyone down!" Jack called.

The cards fell to the bed and lay there like normal cards.

There was a knock on the door.

"Come in," I called.

Mom stepped inside with Curtis, a man who worked with my dad at MIT. He was another brainy guy—Dad once explained that he was "an expert on the math that governs the motions of the tiniest particles in the universe"—whatever that means.

"Oh—hi, Nim, so nice to see you!" Mom said, a pleased expression on her face.

"Hi, Mrs. Kapadia." Nim gave her sweet and innocent for-parents-only smile.

"May we ask you a question?" Mom asked.

"Sure," I replied. I stood up and began to gather up the cards.

Curtis was leaning against the doorjamb, his forefinger to his lips. For some reason he often looked like he was posing for a photo. His thick hair, dark and flecked with silver, lay smoothly on his head like the fur of a chinchilla.

"Did you happen to see a pickup truck when you were walking to school this morning?" Mom asked.

"I don't know," I replied. "Maybe." I was aware of Curtis watching me very closely. He was fidgeting with the pen in his shirt pocket, and he still had that strange air of posing.

"Let us know if you do," Curtis said.

I didn't reply. As I finished picking up the cards, Curtis's eyes grew darker. Then he turned and lumbered out of the room.

"Who is he to tell me what to do?" I asked.

Mom stood facing me. Her mouth opened, then closed again. "Paul, Curtis is only trying to help."

"To *help*?! Is that what he's doing here?" I asked, more coldly than I meant to.

Mom glanced at Nim again, then back at me. "Paul, maybe you should answer a question of mine. What happened in school today?"

"Oh, that," I said.

"Mr. Condor called to say you have an indoor suspension. That's not like you."

"Yeah, I know." I lowered my head.

"Mrs. Kapadia, those guys are terrible bullies. I mean they're awful. Paul's the first person who's been brave enough to fight back," Nim put in.

"It's good of you to stand up for Paul," Mom told her. "But it takes two to tango." She turned her gaze on me.

"I should have controlled my anger better," I admitted.

"I'm glad you realize that. Dad and I have tried to help you boys learn how to make wise choices."

There was silence.

"I'll try to do better," I told her.

"Good. Oh, and Paul," she said, with just the hint of a smile, "can you and Sam go easy on the Epoisses? I'm glad you finally like it—but the two of you almost wiped out a whole wheel of cheese that I was saving for my book group."

Mom's gaze rested on my face a moment, disappointed but gentle, and then she was gone.

I packed the cards into their box and tucked them in my shirt pocket.

"I wish my mom was that nice," Nim commented. "She would have grounded me for a month."

"I'd rather be grounded than feel how much I disappointed her," I replied.

"Parents always play the card that hurts the most," Nim said. "I better go."

By the lamps in my room, her eyes looked light brown, with little flecks of light and dark, like cut stone. I felt a shiver somewhere inside. "Paul . . . *was* there a pickup truck?" she asked.

"Yeah, there was," I said.

"Then why didn't you tell your mom?"

"I don't know. I don't trust that guy Curtis."

She made a little face. "He doesn't look that bad to me. Is it okay if I message you later? Just to check in?"

"Sure."

"K." And she was gone.

15

A year or so ago, when Mom was painting my room, she had me clean out everything—even the stuff in my closet. Mom's the sort of person who believes that the inside of a closet should look as nice as a real room. So I carried out box after box, and after I had carried out the last one, I found a little picture of my Dad on the floor. I'm pretty sure I drew it back when I was three or four. A few squiggly lines for the body, a round face, two eyes, a smiling mouth. The skin colored in dark. I laughed out loud when I first saw the picture, but later that night, as I lay awake in bed, I thought about it again, and for some reason it left me feeling empty and cold. That picture meant so much to me when I drew it, and I hadn't even bothered to take care of it.

That was how it felt now with Dad gone, only a thousand times worse. Because this time it wasn't just a picture, it was Dad himself—his warmth, his laughter, his easy way of talking with us.

Tonight I let my memories of Dad swirl around me, in whatever order they happened to arrive.

Dad shuffling the cards with a satisfying snap at the little table in front of the fire.

His peaceful, comforting voice.

Dad eating according to Indian custom, with his right hand. He could even look neat and elegant when he ate yogurt that way.

The foods that he (and we) loved—samosas, chicken tandoori, spicy dhal, kebabs, curry dishes.

The way he filled up the room with his Dadness.

An old, dark, polished stone—a fossil of some ancient life form—that he carried, he said, to remind himself how short our own lives really are.

Dad styling in a tuxedo and looking pleased when he was going out to a fancy event with Mom.

Telling Mom how beautiful she was.

Dad laughing at his own driving. Saying he was the only man in Massachusetts who couldn't parallel park.

Dad loving the Red Sox and talking about their fielding and their teamwork.

Dad raising his index finger and saying, You can always find your way to an answer. Don't let fear stop you.

Dad picking up Brinda and holding her awkwardly in his lap and telling her how important she was to us all.

Dad telling Sam and me at bedtime that he loved us. And telling us to listen with our hearts as we were falling asleep, and to feel the universe in all its silent splendor. Which I had never been able to do, though sometimes I tried.

Dad asking me, Do you know how I would like to come back in my next life?

As a plum.

16

Late that evening, Jack met with Sam and me. He had talked to the Kings and Queens about Nim's idea, and they agreed with her that salt water would severely disable the scissors people, in the same way it destroyed high-tech devices such as cell phones. Meanwhile, on the other side of the bay, the Aces had found an unusual hole in the sand, and after secretly observing it, they discovered it was the opening to the bunker where the scissors people rested. All the scissors people but a few scattered guards would be sleeping there tonight. Apparently they had to remain attached to their power generator until morning in order to recover the energy that they had expended during the attack.

"We have a short window of opportunity. The time to attack is now!" Jack declared, striking his tiny right fist into the palm of his left hand.

I looked at Sam, and he gave the thumbs up. "We're in!" I replied.

Jack turned to Sam. "Would you be so kind as to transport us across the harbor in your boat?"

Sam bent forward and swept his arm along the floor. "My skiff is your skiff," he said, in his best fake British accent.

Instead of going to bed, I stayed up late. I was determined to track down HOBO. It was hard to make much progress because the message had been specially designed to leave no return email address. The HOBO had to be someone with real computer skills—some hacker—and I couldn't figure out what he or she or it was trying to accomplish. Scare us? Add to our misery? Give us a warning? And why?

Doing a google search about HOBO just brought up pictures of homeless guys and some articles about the Great Depression.

I was still awake when the town clock in North Church struck twelve times. In the dark, the deep clangs of the brass bell sounded huge and round—golden balls of sound that bounced off the rooftops and wobbled off into the night.

Sam and Brinda joined me at the top of the back stairway. As we sneaked down the worn wooden steps, I checked to make sure I had the cards in my pocket. Sam was carrying Brinda, and she was licking one of his hands to thank him for being included.

I unlatched the back door and we crept into the yard. I picked up the two buckets I'd set out there earlier, and we pushed through the gate onto Milk Street. My legs shook a little.

In my mind I was picturing sharp-pointed scissors, hovering in the night air like a school of barracudas. My footsteps slowed and stopped.

"Paul?" Sam whispered to me from ahead.

"Coming," I replied.

I forced myself to focus on what was in front of me. In the middle of the night, everything was different. Even a neighbor's rose garden looked mysterious. Sounds that you couldn't hear during the day were loud. A fountain rippled and splashed somewhere—yet I'd never noticed it before. Clouds were the craziest of all. In the moonlight they looked heavy and 3-D, like ships sailing the heavens—and almost close enough to touch. The breeze was softer and smoother than any breeze during the day.

We stole from street lamp to street lamp along a side street that curved down to the water. As we approached the shore, the trees fell away, and stars spread over us, bright and silvery, like shiny pebbles flung across the sky by an absent-minded giant.

Sam stopped and lifted his arms. "Behold!" he announced.

"What's wrong?" I asked, as a spasm of fear shot through me.

"Orion." Sam turned in a slow circle, stopped, and pointed. "Over there in the south. In a week or two it will be gone; we won't see it again till next winter." He pointed out the constellation—a pattern of bold, straight lines, very clear and beautiful.

"Is that what Dad meant by 'silent splendor'?" I asked.

"Beats me." He glanced about. "Okay, where's that darn boat rack?"

Dad had given Sam his skiff about a year earlier, and they used to go out fishing or scalloping on weekends.

We lifted the skiff off its rack, turned it right side up, and dragged it down to the water. Blades of beach grass stirred in the breeze.

Sam rolled up his pants, took off his shoes, and placed the shoes and the oars in the skiff. "Go ahead, climb in," he ordered me, and once I was settled, he sloshed out into the ice-cold water and pushed the boat away from shore. No complaints about the cold. He loved his boat even more than he loved Portuguese toast with butter and jam.

When the water was nearly up to his knees, Sam hopped in and took his place on the middle seat, facing the stern. He set the oars in their locks and began to row quickly and pretty powerfully, for a little kid.

We glided past some anchored boats and moved out into the open water.

I scanned the sky anxiously, looking for glints of light that might be the reflections from razor-sharp blades. Jack had said that *most* of the scissors people were asleep tonight. But not *all*. There were still some scattered guards around somewhere. What if one of the guards caught sight of us? Would we have time to dive under a seat before they came shooting down?

A pearly cloud sailed in front of the moon and soaked up most of the light.

I set the deck down on the seat, and Jack and some other cards wiggled out of the box and strolled about, peering into the darkness.

The King and the Queen of Spades stood beside me, waiting anxiously for the return of the Aces, who had flown ahead to check out the scissors people's bunker one more time.

Jack hopped up beside us, and the King of Spades began to question him about something. I could make out a few snatches of the conversation: *suspended animation* and *no chance of detection* were two of the phrases I heard.

Sam brought the skiff within sight of the dark shoreline. Brinda started to moan in anticipation. The boat scraped up onto the shore and Sam hopped out and set the anchor in the sand. "This land here is known as the Haul-over," he said quietly and proudly to no one in particular, "because fishermen used to haul their boats across it to the ocean. It was a shortcut."

The beach rose to a ridge of bushes and twisted, gnarly trees. In the distance the roof of one solitary summer home cut a triangular hole in the night sky.

All the cards were now standing on the bow—all forty-eight (everyone but the Aces), from the youngest right up to the Queens and Kings. Sensing the importance of the occasion, even the little ones stood silently, awaiting their orders. Their faces were in shadow, and they were shivering in anticipation.

I was holding Brinda in my arms. All at once she let out a bark—she does that when she's nervous—and I shushed her.

Jack climbed up onto the prow and took his place in front of the cards.

"The Kings and Queens have authorized me to announce the plan," he orated. He called everyone's attention to a line of shells on the beach. "The Aces have gathered those shells for our use. They will be used to transport our crucial weapon—sea-water—to the bunker." He paused.

The Nine of Clubs was hopping up and down. "Sir, sir!" she called.

Jack turned toward her. "Yes?" he asked, in a kindly tone.

"Sir, I don't believe we know what a bunker is." Other children on both sides of her nodded in agreement.

"Ah, yes, I should explain," Jack replied. "To you, it will appear to be nothing more than a hole in the side of a sand dune. But the hole leads to a deep tunnel—and far down the tunnel, lined with oyster shells, is the 'bunker,' or underground shelter, where the scissors people are sleeping. It is there that we will deploy our weapon. Each of you will pour your sea-water directly onto a scissors person."

The children looked at each other and nodded. The Nine of Clubs gave a thumbs-up.

Jack continued, "Our two human friends will wait by the bunker until we exit, and then—to disable any scissors that we might have missed—they will pour a final flood of saltwater down the opening. Then—in silence but with haste—we will return to the skiff!"

As he finished, the four Aces fluttered into view like tiny bats and alighted on the gunwale. Leaning forward in silence, the Ace of Spades touched his head to the King of Spades and then to the Queen.

After a brief discussion, Jack took his place again in front of everyone.

"Very well," he said. "The enemy is asleep, the bunker is ready to be assailed, the water vessels are waiting, and—with the blessing of the King and Queen of Hearts—let us begin!"

The cards swarmed off the bow of the boat and hopped down onto the beach, where four rows of small seashells lay ready. Each card bent down, picked up a shell, dipped it into the sea-water, and scurried off across the beach.

The older cards were looking after the younger and helping them on their way. They ran off: paper-thin rectangles carrying chubby hemispheres of water before them. It might have looked pretty funny, except it was so deadly serious. The Jacks, Kings, and Queens followed the others, carrying larger shells, also full of water.

I'd only known them for one day, but I felt my heart being tugged along with their little feet.

Sam and I each picked up a bucket, dipped it into the harbor, and hurried after them.

A few minutes later we stood in the beach grass about ten yards from the water. Here, on the side of a dune, was the small opening to the bunker, carefully camouflaged by some driftwood. The card people, with their shells full of sea-water, had disappeared down the tunnel. We were left with moonlight and the gentle lapping of waves on the beach.

Suddenly they returned—skittering up the steep incline on their springy little legs.

"All set!" Jack called. He and the other cards scurried off toward the boat.

I glanced at the hole in the sand. "Ready?" I asked Sam. I leaned over for the bucket.

Then I saw it—a flicker of shadow and light coming up the tunnel.

"Now Sam!" I cried. We grabbed the buckets and emptied them, and the sea-water flooded into the tunnel and washed the vile creature away.

Then we ran.

Sam rowed on. The oars splashed and swirled, and stars spun slowly overhead. Lights from the town gleamed through the thick darkness. Each pinpoint of light on shore cast a long, wavering line across the water.

Somewhere in the air above us, I knew, there might be small formations of scissors, locating our little boat in the ripples of light, then banking and descending at a great speed with their sharp blades pointed at our chests. I felt an impulse to duck down out of sight—and I fought it.

Jack hopped back onto my shoulder and said hello. I told him about the scissors person in the tunnel. "I think we took care of him," I said. Jack gave me the thumbs up.

The King of Spades was gesturing to Jack. "Where are the Aces?" he asked, in a husky voice.

"They're making one final inspection, your majesty," Jack told him.

"They should be here by now," the King grunted.

A few minutes later, three Aces fluttered out of the sky and touched down on the seat. The Ace of Spades touched heads again with the King and Queen of Spades.

"This can't be good news," moaned Jack. He hopped off my shoulder and hurried to the King.

A few minutes later Jack hopped back onto my shoulder. "The scissors people caught the Ace of Diamonds," he said, in a trembling voice. "Apparently a few of the guards found him just outside the tunnel . . . and they cut him to pieces." He shivered.

"I'm so sorry," I said.

"That brings us down to fifty-one," Jack said, shaking his head, "and no hope of regenerating."

"No hope of what?"

"Regenerating," he repeated. "Creating copies of ourselves."

"Can that be done?" I asked.

"We're strictly forbidden."

"Forbidden? By who?" I asked.

"We don't know," Jack replied.

A few minutes later we landed and struck out toward home under the dark, glittery sky. As we rounded a corner I heard something clanking, metal on metal—an eerie, empty sound. A spasm of fear shot through me. Was it the guard scissors, lurking in the shadows for us?

I gazed wildly around. Then I saw it: just a flagpole, rattling in the wind.

17

Our night was not yet over.

When we reached our corner, Sam started across the street, but I lunged forward and yanked him back.

"Get down!" I whispered to him. Sam scooped up Brinda, and we crouched down behind a bush.

In front of our house, a pickup truck was parked, engine running, with two men inside.

"What's wrong? Haven't you ever seen a truck before?" Sam asked me.

"That's the truck I saw this morning," I explained.

His mouth began to open and shut soundlessly.

One door creaked open, and a man climbed out and crept toward our house, bent over low. He edged up to a window, raised himself on his elbows, and peered inside.

"What are we afraid of?" Sam asked. "That's our property. Those guys are trespassers." He raised himself to his feet.

"Get down, Sam!" I yanked him down again.

The guy at the window turned and gestured. The second door creaked open, and the other guy joined him under a tree. They stood there a few minutes, talking.

Brinda had been watching the men. She had begun to growl, louder and more fiercely.

When my brother has one of his ideas, he doesn't stop to ask if anyone else approves of it.

He set Brinda down on the ground and cried, "Go get 'em, girl!"

Brinda hobbled across the street with her old-dog run. She's lost most of her speed, but she hasn't lost her voice. She started baying at full volume, like a hound on a rabbit hunt.

Lights turned on up and down the street.

The men hurried back to the truck and hopped in. Brinda shuffled toward them, still barking like a fiend. It was probably fortunate that it was too dark for the men to see how little she really was.

The truck started up with a roar and lurched away down the road.

Brinda gave chase for half a block, then stopped and returned to us with her slow, off-kilter victory trot.

She accepted our caresses and praise the way a Nobel Peace Prize winner might accept the medal placed around her neck.

Before I went to bed I decided to check the emails one more time, and there it was, another new message waiting for me—again with no return email address.

For those in peril, help arrives.

But meddling friends often pay with their lives.

—HOBO

My heart began to race. Another threat. What did it mean by "meddling friends"? Me and Sam? Curtis? Or did it mean other friends, like Nim, who were starting to help?

At that moment I glanced up. Something had caught my eye.

That faint light flickering in the square above the monitor. Wasn't that the spot where they had the camera on these computers? I bent in closer for a better look, and the light immediately guttered out.

I slammed my fist on my knee.

Had someone been watching us?

And that someone was most likely the HOBO.

I found a piece of black electrical tape and stuck it in place over the camera. So much for that. But how much had they already learned about us and the card people? How much damage had already been done?

The cards had stacked themselves up in a neat pile next to me. I put them in their box, placed them under my pillow, and tried without much success to fall asleep.

18

The assistant principal, Mr. Condor, was a youngish, bald guy with pink skin and bad coffee breath. After another night with little sleep, it wasn't that bad to spend my indoor suspension in his office. There was schoolwork for me from all the different teachers. I finished it early and spent the rest of the day reading *To Kill a Mockingbird*.

At one point, my English teacher Ms. Burns looked in on me and smiled. "Don't you love this book?" she asked. She's young and pretty and extremely lively.

"Yes," I said, looking at the floor.

"We'll see you in a couple days, okay?"

"Okay."

"Paul, can you meet my eyes?"

I looked up.

"Be proud of who you are. Nobody has the power to take that away from you."

She was so nice, it sort of hurt.

Her footsteps echoed down the hall, and I turned back to the book. I guess I fell asleep, because Mr. Condor had to wake me at the final bell.

I was out in front of the school, and still a little groggy, when someone bumped into me from the side.

"Oh, sorry," he said, real sarcastic. It was one of Butch and Ken's big goony eighth grade friends.

Someone else bumped me harder, from behind, and knocked me flat.

The two of them stepped around me, laughing.

"That's for getting our friends in trouble," one of them called back over his shoulder. He added some choice insults about me and my family.

That was it. No more Mr. Nice Guy.

I picked myself up and brushed myself off.

"Hey—you wanna fight? Bring it on!" I called after them. Probably not the wisest thing to say, under the circumstances. But Dad had told me, Don't give in to fear. "Come on—bring it on!" I repeated.

I expected them to turn around and charge me. I made sure the deck of cards was securely tucked away in an inside pocket. I braced myself.

But they just kept right on going, strutting off like roosters. One of them held up his left hand over his head with only the middle finger raised.

19

Nim was waiting for me at the corner, and I filled her in on the trip to the Haul-over and the deployment of our secret weapon—sea-water. "That was your idea," I reminded her.

She smiled, but then her brow furrowed. "That's great . . . But did it work?"

"We don't know yet. The Aces will snoop around and find out." Then I told her about the death of the Ace of Diamonds.

She grabbed me by the arm. "Listen to me, Paul. Do you feel safe?"

I shuddered. "No, I don't feel safe." She was watching me closely. "But so what?" I added. Maybe the way I stood up to those eighth graders had given me a little extra strength. "I'm not letting down my friends. And I'm not letting down Dad."

Her amber eyes widened a notch. She nodded. "Okay. Okay, then."

As we turned down Milk Street toward my house, my stomach sank. There was Curtis again, standing in the yard with Mom. They were holding onto her old bicycle and looking it over.

"Hi, honey," Mom chirped. "Hi, Nim." I could hear it in her voice: the sadness and fear under the cheeriness. What was Curtis doing there? It didn't make any sense.

"Hi, Mrs. Kapadia," Nim chirped back. "Hi, Curtis."

"Hello," he replied in a voice that was way too serious. He had a sweater tied around his neck like someone posing for a magazine ad about drugs for old people with high cholesterol or ED.

"Curtis is fixing my bike for me," Mom said. "I'm about to try it out."

"That's nice," I replied, pretty sarcastic.

"I don't think Curtis is so bad," Nim told me when we were inside. "He's just sort of a dork."

"He gives me the creeps," I retorted. "Speaking of which, I have something really creepy to show you. I'm getting these messages from someone who calls himself HOBO—"

"HOBO?" Lines wrinkled her forehead. "Can I see?"

I put the deck of cards on my bed and opened the laptop. She read both HOBO messages and said she thought they were from someone who wanted to help, but couldn't for some reason.

That was pure Nim—always looking for the best in people.

"I don't think so. Here's something even worse—I think they've been watching us." I showed her the piece of black tape that I used to cover the flickering light at the top of the monitor.

She looked skeptical. "I don't think people can do that, Paul. I don't think they can get inside your computer's camera."

We argued about it awhile.

Finally she said, "Paul, you know, you've changed since . . . all this," she said.

I turned toward her. "I have?"

"In good ways," she assured me. "I mean, I know you withdrew for a while, but when you came back, you were different. You were braver. You stood up to Butch and those guys. Which you never did before."

I nodded. "Yeah, I guess that's true."

Then her brow furrowed. "But look, Paul . . . I hope you aren't going to get paranoid on us. The light in the top of your computer flickering? I mean, come on!" She gave me a little push on the shoulder, and this time I didn't flinch.

Before I could start arguing again, Nim changed the subject. She glanced over at the bed. "They're learning so quickly!" she exclaimed. The card people had woken up and were starting to play. The littlest ones were flopping down on the bedspread, doing flips, then bouncing back up to their feet. In the middle of all this unhappiness and worry, their laughter was like the sound of new leaves turning over in the sunshine.

20

In no time Nim was back to work on her construction project. She cut out some more shapes and began to assemble them. Whatever she was making had several compartments. By now, the card children trusted her with the scissors and didn't stop their play.

As Nim was finishing up, Jack hopped onto my shoulder. "I believe that the Clubs are ready to test their new form of transportation. Would you mind opening the window?"

"First take a look at what I've done." Nim smiled at him.

"Of course," Jack replied politely.

It was a little house. In typical Nim fashion, quietly and without any fanfare, she had created the shell of a two-story structure, complete with stairs, windows, and six different rooms. She set the home on the bed in front of Jack, and he climbed all through it, looking here and there and making admiring remarks about the space. "There's even a bed!" he exclaimed.

"Try it out," she told him. "I'll be making some tables and chairs later."

Jack lay down and stretched out on his back. "Wonderfully comfortable," he announced, lifting his little head and smiling at her.

He went off to round up the rest of the cards to show them the house, and they paraded through, buzzing with pleasure.

Then it was time for their transportation test. Nim pushed open the window as requested and came over and took a seat next to me.

The cards had gathered on the desk, not far from the open window. Four of the Clubs—the Jack and three of the older children—huddled nearest the window. They were attached to each other by some sort of light thread, and they wore tiny crash helmets made of pistachio shells.

"On three!" the Jack of Clubs called. "One . . . two . . . three . . ."

At that, they jumped into the air, tilted slightly forward, and floated up into the wind. The Queen of Clubs stood below them on the desk, holding the end of the thread.

"Maintain your angle," she called to them. "No sudden movements."

"Magnificent!" the King of Clubs shouted. "Bravo!"

The cards drifted about on the breeze, a kite composed of four interconnected parts.

You had to hand it to these little guys—their lives were in peril at any given moment, but they just kept moving forward, with all the courage in the world.

In a lot of ways, they were just like Dad.

21

Nim and I watched them conduct some more tests. Then, she turned to me.

"Paul, we need to talk."

I gave her a quick look. "Didn't we just talk?"

"This is something different. I owe you an apology," she said.

"That's okay," I replied.

"It's not okay. I was terrible to you. For months."

"Why?" I was looking down at my hands—the bad habit Mom keeps reminding me about.

She sighed. "This sounds lame, but for all these years I felt on the outside. You know how it was—I was different than all the other kids in Bayview. I was from Thailand. No one in this town had even heard of Thailand."

"I had."

"You were the only one. And I was Asian. I looked different. You were the only one who liked me for who I was. Of course, you were South Asian—or half South Asian."

"We were friends."

"Right. But then I started to get older, and suddenly—I don't know how it happened—but suddenly it was cool to be

Asian. Then that group of kids wanted me to be one of them, and everyone said they were, like, the coolest . . ."

"Did you like being with them?"

"Not really," she said, pushing a strand of hair back behind her ear. "I mean, I pretended to, because I thought that was what I was supposed to do. But the things they talk about . . ."

"What kinds of things?"

"It's really boring, makeup and boys."

"So you're done with all that? Done with makeup and boys?"

"I'm not done with boys," she asserted. She shook back her hair. "I mean, there's a boy I like."

A boy she liked? I hadn't even begun to think about having a girlfriend. "You mean you have a boyfriend?" I asked.

"Not yet."

"Does he go to our school?"

"He's in high school."

I looked away. "Isn't he too old for you?"

"He's nice. He's not at all like those boys who picked on you. But I don't think he even knows who I am." She sighed.

Over the past few months, Nim had definitely changed . . . in a number of ways. In some ways she seemed years older, but in other ways she was still just Nim, the girl who always looked for the best in the world around her—sometimes to the point of ignoring the painful truth right before her eyes.

She took my hands and looked me full in the face. "Will you accept my apology?" she asked. Her eyes looked sad and sincere.

"Yes," I said.

She squeezed my hands. "Thank you."

The door to the room burst open, and the cards immediately collapsed onto the desk.

"Yo," Sam said. "What's going on? Hi, Nim. Hey, where's the card people?"

My heart was racing madly. "Knock next time," I snapped.

He sauntered over, slid between us, and put an arm around our backs. "Just look at you two beautiful young people. Is it really true? Are we friends again?" he asked, smiling his I'm-a-cute-little-brother smile. "Is that what I'm seeing here? Are we all good friends again?"

Nim patted my hand absently and looked at me with a questioning glance.

A dark shape filled the doorway, panting for breath.

"Hurry, boys!" a man shouted. "Your mother!"

"What?" I exclaimed.

"Hurry! She's . . . I called the ambulance . . ."

It was Curtis, and for once he didn't seem to be posing. His hair was mussed, his shirt was dirty, and he looked genuinely confused. Only the ballpoint pen in his shirt pocket—white, with a black cap—seemed to be keeping up appearances as usual. Before we could get up, he turned and slogged clumsily off down the hall.

22

We raced outside—and stopped in our tracks.

Mom was sprawled on her side on the strip of grass between the sidewalk and the street. She wasn't moving.

"It's coming back!" someone—a neighbor—was yelling. In the distance, an angry blast of sound shattered the air.

"Go to Mom!" I told Sam.

I darted out onto the pavement.

It was the same dull red pickup truck that I'd seen yesterday on the way to school. It was already going fast, and as it rumbled toward us it kept building more speed. It took a curve on two wheels and lurched back onto all four, bouncing like a speedboat, and at the last instant it swerved over into the wrong lane—directly towards Mom, towards me, towards all of us.

Just in time I leapt back into some bushes, and the truck roared past, inches away, snapping off branches and smashing down a mailbox. Somehow it swerved around the ambulance that was screaming into view from the opposite direction.

I jumped to my feet and ran over to join Sam, who was kneeling over Mom.

"She's breathing," he said, in a tiny voice.

The ambulance pulled up, and three rescue workers pressed in beside Mom. They pushed Sam and me away and formed a wall around her.

She was moving a little now. She had lifted one arm and was talking in a quiet voice to the rescue worker who knelt beside her. The worker was bandaging her face. Not far away, her bicycle—what was left of it—lay in a heap near a tree. Its frame was twisted like a pretzel.

The red and blue lights of the ambulance spun slowly, splashing purple shadows around the neighborhood.

Curtis came up beside us and did his best to explain, in his strange, stiff way. They had just fixed her bicycle, he said. The second she got on her bike and pedaled out onto the street, the pickup truck came out of nowhere, struck her, and drove off. Hit and run.

"Why they came back is beside me," he said.

"They wanted to make sure they finished the job," Sam announced grimly.

"I was quite surprised." Though Curtis sounded upset and his face was streaked with sweat and dirt, his face looked oddly expressionless. "Did anyone get the license plate?" he asked.

We all looked at each other and shook our heads dumbly.

Nim joined us, and the three of us hovered near Mom. A rescue worker held up a hand: Keep your distance. We could hear Mom moaning.

Slowly, with care, they supported her neck and lifted her onto a stretcher and into the back of the ambulance.

One of the rescue workers turned to us. "Are you her kids?" she asked.

"Yes," I replied. I took a step forward.

"We're taking her to Mass General. Can you get a ride there?" I looked around for Curtis; he was nowhere to be seen.

Nim raised a hand.

"Hi, I'm a friend. My mom can drive them," she declared. She took out her cell phone, punched a few buttons, and walked off to the side while she spoke in Thai. Her voice snapped with authority. "My mom's coming," she announced.

I went over to Sam and rested a hand on his shoulder.

"We're going to lose Mom," he sobbed. "We're going to lose her just like we lost Dad." His body shook like an over-heated engine.

"No we're not," I said fiercely. "We're not going to lose Mom."

"How can you know that?" Sam sobbed. "You can't know that."

The ambulance, with our mother inside, crunched over the loose gravel at the end of the driveway and started off down the street, siren wailing. The pitch kept sliding lower, like the whistle of a train shooting past you on its way to the end of the world.

23

Nim's mother, Rajini, worked in the kitchen of Bayview Acres, a nursing home at the edge of town. Her supervisor let her leave, and she showed up in her old Honda Accord only a few minutes later. She was short and skinny—she probably weighed under a hundred pounds—and as she drove us into Boston, I wondered how she could see over the steering wheel.

The waiting area at the emergency room was pretty crowded, and everyone looked either sick or hurt or worried. Nim talked to a woman behind a desk while we found a place to sit. Rajini took out her knitting. There was nothing to do but wait.

"Where's Curtis?" Nim asked.

I shrugged. I'd almost forgotten about him.

But a few minutes later, Curtis came bumbling in through the entrance, stopped just inside as if posing to have his picture taken, noticed us, and strode over.

"Have you heard anything?" he asked.

I shook my head. Without another word, Curtis took a magazine off the rack and sat down across from us. He seemed relieved to be able to hide between its covers.

"Paul!" Sam whispered.

"What?"

"Look at his pocket!" He motioned with his head toward Curtis.

"What about it?"

"Look at the bulge there." In a tiny voice, Sam added, "I think it's a gun."

It actually did look like the outline of a handgun.

We waited and waited. After a while, Curtis stood up and offered to get everyone food. We all declined. The evening news shows came on. There was a story about Mom's accident and some footage of our street and of an ambulance. Sam covered his face with his hands and started weeping. I put an arm around him.

At some point a policewoman stepped inside, gave a few quick glances around the room, saw us, and strode over. She talked to Sam and me about the accident and asked for details about the truck. Like Curtis, she seemed disappointed that we hadn't caught the license plate. She gave us a sympathetic look, patted our hands, and left.

The hours stretched on.

Finally, around 9:00 pm, a doctor stepped out through the white double doors. She was wearing blue scrubs, and she had pulled her mask down under her chin. She had dirty blond hair and her face was saggy with exhaustion.

"Are there any relatives here for Louise Kapadia?" she asked, looking around the room.

I stood up. "My brother and I. We're her sons," I said. Curtis stirred in his seat but didn't get up.

The doctor nodded. "I'm Dr. Westfield. Would you come this way, please?"

We followed her to the double doors. She led us inside to a desk with a couple of chairs.

She took a seat across from us. "Your mother is going to be all right," she said.

Sam began to cry.

"She escaped major injury. She's fully conscious and aware. She's very, very lucky. But she's had a major concussion, and she'll need lots of rest."

"Thank you," I heard myself saying. The room was melting around me.

"Can we see her?" Sam asked. He was still sniffling.

She smiled. "You may visit her for a very short time." She led us down a hall to a room. She gestured to step inside, then she retreated into the hall and took out her cell phone.

Mom was lying on her back, partly propped up. Her eyes swung toward us. She had a bandage on the top of her head. We approached her cautiously. She motioned for us to lean over her, and she put her arms around us.

"I love you," she said, in a tiny voice.

"We love you, too," we told her.

"Are you all right, Mommy?" Sam asked.

"I'm fine," she said. "Don't you worry about me." Her words were slurred, and her voice was a flat, dull monotone.

She was trying to say something else, and we had to lean closer to hear it.

"Say thank you to Rajini."

"We will, Mom."

Her lips moved again, almost soundlessly. I put my ear up against her lips. "Danger . . ." she was saying. It was like the voice of a little creature from deep inside a seashell. "Danger . . ." Her voice slowed and was still.

"We'll be careful, Mom," I said.

She gazed at us for another minute, and once or twice she opened her mouth like she wanted to speak again, but her eyes closed. She was asleep.

Sam gave me a sad and scared look, and I put my arm around him again.

The doctor reappeared, and as she led us back toward the waiting room, she asked, "By any chance, are you boys related to Samir Kapadia? The computer scientist?"

"He's our father," I said.

"I'm very sorry for your loss. I met him once or twice myself. My husband, David, worked with him at MIT. He had great respect for your father."

"Does he do research into nanotechnology too?" Sam asked.

There was a glimmer behind her eyes. "You two are very knowledgeable," she remarked. "Yes, he does. Now I'm remembering something he told me . . . You live in Bayview year-round, don't you?"

"Yes."

"We know the area well. We have a summer cottage there." She held open the door to the waiting room.

"We may want to talk to your husband sometime, if that's okay," I told her. I wasn't exactly sure why I said it.

"Any time you want," she responded. She seemed to think the request was perfectly normal, given the circumstances. She scrawled something on a pad of paper and ripped off the sheet. "This is our phone number in Cambridge."

"Thank you."

"By the way, I don't mean to interfere, but do you have someone to stay with you tonight?"

"Yes," we said. "Our friend's mother."

The doctor bent forward. "Now don't worry, your mother will be coming home before you know it." She wrinkled her nose in a friendly way.

When we gave Curtis the news about Mom, he pursed his lips and nodded. No other reaction. What was his story? Was he part machine, maybe some sort of cyborg?

Definitely not someone you could trust.

Nim gave Sam and me a hug. She explained to her mother what was going on, and Rajini put away her knitting.

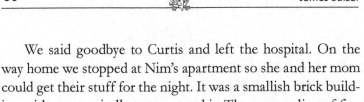

We said goodbye to Curtis and left the hospital. On the way home we stopped at Nim's apartment so she and her mom could get their stuff for the night. It was a smallish brick building with some spindly trees around it. There was a line of five mailboxes by the front door—five apartments in one small building! For the first time, I wondered what Nim might have thought over the years about the difference between my home and hers.

A few minutes later she and her mother came downstairs with their overnight bags, and Rajini drove us to our house.

The headlights caught Mom's trashed bicycle, still lying in a sad heap by the tree. Someone, maybe the police, had put a big piece of yellow tape around the handlebars. Before I went inside, I picked up the bike and carried into the back yard and hid it behind the shed so we wouldn't have to look at it anymore.

But as I fell asleep that night, the bent curves of the bicycle danced before my eyes, and once or twice they morphed into the dark handles of a pair of large and lethal scissors.

24

The next morning we received two pieces of good news.

The Aces had discovered that the sea-water had worked as planned. It had caused serious damage to the scissors people, and it would be a few days before they could regain their power.

And there was great news from the hospital. Mom would be coming home that afternoon.

It was Saturday—no school. Rajini helped us get breakfast, and then she left for her morning shift at the nursing home. Once she was gone, the card people started cleaning up the bits of cardboard left on the floor from Nim's construction project. Again they used the bent ends of Q-tips as push brooms. Sam came in and watched as I scooped up the piles and threw them away.

"I wish Dad could see this," Sam said, gesturing fondly toward the card people. He lay back on my bed and started to play a game on his phone.

"Can't you make yourself useful for a change?" I snapped at him.

"What'd I do wrong?" Sam asked in a hurt voice.

I heard Mom's voice in my head, asking me how I was treating my brother.

But the truth is, that kid is *lazy*.

There was something I'd been thinking about, and I called Jack over for a discussion.

"We need to have a secret code if you're ever in trouble," I told him. "There might be times when you have to pretend to be a normal old deck of cards."

Jack agreed, and for the next few minutes we discussed some key phrases and what they would mean.

Later that morning, Jack invited us to watch the card people test their new kite-powered transportation out in the big world. Their airfield of choice was the parking lot at Children's Beach, an open and windy area near the shore. I brought the card people in my pocket, and Sam carried a small pouch with their extra equipment. Nim brought along a spool of thread.

Once we made sure the coast was clear, the card people came out of hiding. They milled about on the pavement, talking and enjoying their time outside—all but the Clubs, who got right to work.

Under the direction of the Ten and Jack, the Clubs children connected themselves to each other by short pieces of thread and arranged themselves into a neat formation. Sam handed something to the Queen of Clubs that looked like a tiny scooter. Before you knew it, they were ready.

The other cards stood off to one side, commenting on the cleverness of the Clubs.

"It is time," announced the King of Clubs, who was not nearly as long-winded as the other Kings.

The Clubs children fanned out and turned to face the wind. The Queen stood on her scooter upwind of them, connected to them by a long piece of thread. At her signal the cards leapt into the air, caught the brisk wind, and rose up into the sky. The thread that bound them to the Queen stretched and held as she stood, motionless, on her scooter. Then she released her

brake, and the card people kite sailed off before the wind—
pulling along the scooter (with the Queen on board) across the
pavement toward shore.

Some of the cards cheered and bumped fists. The Diamond
children began to chant, "It works! It's green! It's so good, it's
obscene!"

Sam was frowning. "Did you know Dad and I sometimes
flew a kite from the skiff to see if the wind could pull us?" he
asked me. "Which it did, by the way."

"What's that got to do with anything?" I asked back.

"I don't know." He gave me a hurt look.

At the far end of the parking lot, the Queen pressed down
the brake to stop the scooter. The airborne Clubs dipped
and swiveled, trying to lose their air so they could drop to
the ground. But at the wrong moment a strong gust of wind
whooshed over us, and the Clubs shot up higher into the air.

"Oh geez!" Sam exclaimed.

The thread to the scooter pulled tight, tighter, tighter still
. . . and it snapped.

The kite sailed off before the wind.

25

The tiny band of Clubs fluttered away over the sand dunes towards the bay. The Hearts, Diamonds and Spades oohed and cried out in fear. Somewhere in the distance I could hear the Jack and Ten of Clubs trying to take charge, reminding the older children to keep a tight grip on the younger children and lean upwind. But in seconds they were all carried away, out of sight and sound, over a sand dune.

"OMG, we have to find them!" Nim cried, scooping up the other cards with Sam's help.

I grabbed Jack and tucked him in my shirt pocket, and we raced across the sand.

We came to the top of a small hill and stopped to take a look. Ahead of us, the white beach gleamed in the sun, and the blue bay stirred in the breeze. A fishing boat cut a wake through the channel. There was nothing else . . . except on the next hill over, a boy sat facing the water, strumming his guitar and singing.

"Did they land in the water?" Sam asked.

"I hope not," I replied, looking for Nim to see what she thought.

But Nim had slipped away. She was hurrying across the sand toward the guy with the guitar. Sam and I glanced at each other, shrugged, and ran after her.

"Hi," Nim called, waving her hand. We caught up to her as the guitarist stopped strumming and turned toward her.

"Hey, Nim!" he said. He gave a wide, handsome smile. "What're you doin' here!"

"How you doin'?" she asked. I could hear something new in her voice—something older and breathier. She stopped just a few yards from him.

"What's up?" he asked.

"Nothing much." She shook her hair. "Just hangin' out. What's up with you?"

"Oh . . . just writing a new song," he said. "Or trying to." He strummed a chord. He was definitely older than us—a high school kid. He had long, dark brown hair and his nose and eyebrows were made of straight, easy lines. He wore jeans and a white T-shirt. He looked pretty strong. He saw Sam and me and gave a little wave.

"I'm glad you're writing more songs. I love your songs," Nim said. She swayed a little on her feet and pulled a strand of her hair back behind her ears. "Oh, these are my friends . . . Paul and Sam." She had slipped her feet out of her sandals. She flexed the arches of her feet and wiggled her toes in the warm sand.

"Hey. I'm Lex," the boy said.

"Have you seen any cards?" Sam asked.

"Um, do you mean running across the moors? Like on their way to jump in and go for a little swim?" Lex asked.

"Yeah, maybe," Sam replied. "That could've been them. You saw 'em?"

I hit Sam on the shoulder, maybe a little too hard. He gave me an angry look.

Nim laughed. "Funny, huh?" she said.

"My brother has a weird imagination," I said. "We lost some cards, that's all."

"I don't know," Lex said, "something fluttered by a minute ago. I thought it was, like, a bird or something. Maybe it was your cards. It landed somewhere down there." He pointed down the hill, toward some bushes. "How'd they get away from you?"

"Thanks," I said. I started down the hill, followed by Sam.

"We were playing fifty-two pickup," I heard Nim explain.

"Not a good idea on a windy day," Lex replied.

"No, it wasn't. Well . . . thanks," Nim told him.

"Hope you find 'em," Lex said. "Hey, I'll see you around, okay?"

"Anytime you want," she told him. Then she was sprinting after us.

A loud blast of sound followed us. Lex was blowing on something. "Just my kazoo!" he called, and he laughed. He blew on it again, a big trumpet blast. Nim laughed also, very loudly, and waved at him again.

We came down one hill, up another, and down the second . . . and there we found them. The cards had come down in a bayberry bush. They were all tangled up in the branches and in the clusters of waxy gray-green berries.

Jack ran down my arm and hopped onto the bush.

"Any and all help greatly appreciated!" the Ten of Clubs called from the middle of a leafy branch, where he was trying to rescue one of the younger children.

Sam and I untangled some of the children while Nim went off to look for strays. Three of the younger ones had already jumped down onto the sand and were toddling about happily. Nim bent over and picked them up and let them climb up her arms and into her hair.

"Glad I found you. You left your sandals back there," a voice said. The voice came closer. "Whoa! What in the world . . ."

The cards all flopped down. The ones on the bayberry bush went lifeless in the branches. The little ones fell flat onto Nim's arms. A few cards floated through the air and landed gently on the sand.

But it was too late. Lex stood there, in plain sight, his guitar dangling at his side.

"Those cards really *do* have arms and legs!" he exclaimed.

Nim looked toward me. I was shaking my head.

"Naw," I said. "Not really. That was an optical illusion."

He lifted up his guitar, peered at it closely, and brushed some sand off it. He tucked it under his arm. "Not a chance," he said.

We stared at him in silence.

"They had arms and legs, and they were, like, walking around," Lex went on.

"There's a reason for that," Nim told him.

She looked toward me and made a little face. An apology. "The reason is . . . they're alive."

Lex looked in silence from Nim to me and back again to Nim.

"Unless there's something truly bad going on here, like these guys are a threat to national security or something," he said, "you can trust me to keep your secret."

Sam had been watching him closely. "I trust you," he said.

Suddenly, I felt everyone's eyes on me.

"All right," I said. "We'll tell you what we know, but you have to keep totally quiet about it. And I mean totally."

For good or bad, I knew we would be seeing a lot more of this guy Lex.

26

That afternoon Nim helped us get ready for Mom. I washed Mom's sheets, made her bed, and vacuumed the rug in her room. Sam cleaned the sink and put new soap in the shower dish. Nim cut up fruit and sprinkled it with sugar and put it in a bowl with plastic wrap on top. Sam printed out a "Welcome Home!" banner on the computer, and I took my savings out of my piggybank, walked down to the flower shop, and came back with a dozen roses.

A number of adults stopped me along the way and asked me about my mother, and all I had to say was, "My mom is coming home from the hospital today," and they smiled and nodded and sent their love. Small-town New England, everyone knew everything about everyone else.

From time to time I patted the deck of cards in my pocket to make sure it was still there.

Sam and I were both near tears all afternoon. Nim looked over the house one last time, pronounced it good enough for the homecoming, and left.

We sat and waited for Curtis to bring Mom home.

Late that afternoon gravel crunched in the driveway, and the red Prius pulled up. We ran outside.

Curtis had opened the door on the passenger's side and was helping Mom get out.

"Mommy!" Sam called, running up to her. I followed close behind.

Mom stood up, slowly and stiffly. She turned her head carefully and gazed around her, as if trying to make sure that this was really her home.

We ran up and buried our heads against her.

"I love you," she said. She kissed us.

"We love you too," we murmured. I was aware of Curtis standing there awkwardly.

"We got the house ready for you, Mommy," Sam said.

"Have you been safe?" she asked. We nodded. For a moment her eyes lingered on us; then she turned and trudged painfully, like an old, old lady, toward the house.

Sam flashed me a scared look.

Curtis was still standing beside his car. "Okay if I come in?" he asked.

I just looked at him for a minute. "Umm . . . I think we should just keep Mom really quiet. No visitors for now."

"You sure you don't need any help with your mom?"

"We're fine."

"Well, okay," he said. His eyebrows rose in the middle like black caterpillars. "Okay. If that's what you want."

I didn't answer. Curtis climbed back into his car, and it glided silently into the dusk.

When I came inside, I found Mom and Sam still at the bottom of the stairs. Mom was leaning over, holding onto the railing.

Sam flashed me another scared look. "I can't get her up the stairs," he told me.

I came over, we both took an arm, and we half-guided, half-lifted her up the stairs. From there she was able to shuffle into her room.

Mom smiled at the vase of roses on her dresser. Sam had set the bowl of fruit on the little table next to the bed, and he found some extra pillows for her to lean against. We helped her into bed.

"Thank you, boys, I'm very comfortable." She swung her eyes over to watch me carry her bag into the room. "Where's Curtis?"

"He left."

"Oh." She regarded me for a moment. "Everything okay?"

"It's fine, Mom."

Mom sat and chatted with us for a minute, then said she was tired. "You won't mind if I take a nap now, will you?" she asked.

We told her of course not, and she leaned back and fell immediately asleep. We looked at each other. It was much worse than we expected. It was going to take time, and lots of it.

27

Sunday morning a new message arrived:

A Further Thought.
When your heart is battered and you're on your knees
You need to find someone with true expertise.
—HOBO

I never knew what to expect from the HOBO. This email sounded almost sympathetic. But why? And what sort of expertise would we need?

I wanted to grab this HOBO by the shoulders and shake him, or her, or it.

Mom didn't look so good. Her face was swollen and her eyes kept drifting to the side like she didn't have real control over them. When she tried to talk to us, her thoughts jumped from one topic to the next. And she looked worried. Sam kept sending me I-can't-believe-this glances. More than once, I saw her gazing out the window. Then, without warning, her head fell back on her pillow and she was asleep.

"That accident has made her freaky," Sam whispered as we left the room.

"She'll be okay," I replied.

"What if she's not?" Sam asked.

"Don't be negative."

"I can be whatever I want."

I gave him a little shove.

Wham! He punched my shoulder.

I stopped and turned to him. "What was that for?" I asked.

"Stop pushing me and hitting me!" he screamed. He stomped his feet like an angry muffin.

"What are you talking about?" I asked.

"You keep yanking me around and dissing me! I'm telling you to cut it out!" he snarled.

"You're acting like a moron," I told him.

"You're the moron!" he exclaimed, and he stalked off to his room and slammed the door behind him.

I sat down at my desk, thinking, *What a little twerp.*

But after a while I realized, okay, maybe I *had* been a little rough on Sam. It wasn't his fault that he was too young to know how to deal with all this stuff—Dad's disappearance, Mom's accident. The scissors people. Maybe I needed to go a little gentler on him.

At that moment there was a knock on the door, and it pushed open slowly. "I hope I didn't hurt you," Sam said. He peered toward me, real concern on his face.

It would have been an insult to tell him he hadn't hurt me, so I replied, "I guess I deserved it."

"You got that right!" he declared.

He sat down on a chair, frowned importantly, and opened up his laptop.

And that was that. That's the way brothers apologize.

By the time Nim joined us a bit later in the morning, the cards had arranged themselves around the bedroom in four separate groups. The Spades were discussing the differences between animal life and card people life. The Clubs were building small, wheeled vehicles. The Hearts were having wrestling matches and playing a game that looked like charades. And the Diamonds . . . well, they were mainly looking at themselves in the mirror on my dresser, commenting on their shape and attractiveness.

Nim watched them and couldn't stop smiling. I had an idea that she was smiling for some other reason, too—like, maybe, a guy with a guitar.

After another minute I was able to ask her. "Is he the boy?"

"Who?" Nim came back.

"Lex. Is he the boy you told me about?"

Blood rushed to her face. "Yes," she replied.

That was a conversation-stopper.

28

Nim was hard at work again on more cardboard creations for the card people. She had just finished a spacious conference room with a large round table, and now she was putting together dozens of little chairs.

The Hearts and Spades children were watching her cut and glue, and they oohed and aahed in pleasure.

"Thank you so much!" the Eight of Hearts exclaimed.

"You are so quick!" the Seven of Spades marveled.

A few Diamonds children stood at the table, pretending to give speeches on matters of earth-shaking importance.

Nearby, the Clubs children were holding hands and shrieking. They had just discovered that an electrical current pulsed through them when they held hands in a circle.

While Nim worked, I searched the internet for any traces of Dad. Scientists' chat rooms, that sort of thing.

Eventually I came to a site on nanotechnology, and I found something there that caught my attention. A number of speeches and articles were by a Dr. David Westfield from MIT . . . That had to be the husband of the doctor in the hospital. And it was strange, because some of his papers seemed to be about the *impossibility* of nanotechnology. His argument (which some other scientists disputed) was that the chemical bonds inside molecules were too strong to allow computers to be built on a sub-atomic scale. I showed the article to Nim, and she shook her head.

"Pretty confusing," she said.

Sorting through the things on my desk, I picked up a pen and stared at it. A white ballpoint pen with a black cap.

It was all too familiar.

I turned to Nim and Sam.

"Look at this!" I exclaimed. I held it up.

"I believe that is called a pen," Sam replied. He pursed his lips and jabbed a forefinger at me. "They are more common than you might imagine."

"Don't you know where this came from?"

There was a pause.

"Did the stork bring it?" Sam asked.

"Don't you get it?"

"Get what?" Sam gave me a clueless look.

Nim looked toward me, her eyes narrowed.

"Who always carries this type of pen around? Like every day of his life?" I continued.

"I don't know . . . Curtis?" Sam asked.

"Yes. He's obsessed with these pens."

"So what?" Sam asked.

"Well, how did it get here? Don't you see? What if Curtis has been snooping around in my room? Remember how he was late getting to the hospital?"

Nim was shaking her head. "Paul . . ." she began.

"And what if he told the guys in the pickup truck that Mom was about to try out her bike?" I continued.

"No way," Nim cut in. "Curtis likes your mother. He would never try to hurt her."

I shrugged. "Maybe, maybe not. How else would this pen get into my room?" I asked.

"And anyway, what makes you think Curtis knows anything about the cards?" Nim asked.

I tried to think back over the events of the past few days.

"When Curtis saw us with the cards the other day . . . I don't know, his eyes got darker or something," I said.

"People's eyes don't get darker, Paul."

"Wait a minute!" Sam cut in. "Maybe Paul's right. For one thing, Curtis carries a gun—we saw that in the hospital. And second, he's like, a cyborg, or something. Even if he turns out by some miracle to be human, he's got to be on the wrong side."

"Dad said he had enemies at work. This all makes perfect sense," I replied.

"Man! And Mom's been bringing him into our house," Sam continued. "He tricked Mom into thinking he was trying to help."

"Hold on, you guys. You two are getting *way* ahead of yourselves," Nim cautioned. "What makes you so sure that Curtis is evil? I just think he's sort of awkward." She chewed on a piece of her hair.

"Why would Dad's enemies hate these cards?" I wondered aloud.

"Because the cards want to destroy the scissors people!" Sam declared.

"Yes, that's it!" I agreed. "Curtis invented the scissors people. He wants them to triumph, so that nanotechnology can create even bigger and scarier weapons in the future."

Nim shook her head again. "You two are crazy."

29

"I know what we need to do," I said.

Nim held up her hand to stop, but I ignored her.

"You know the doctor? The one who took care of Mom that first night?" I went on.

"Yeah, Dr. Westbrook or something. She was really nice," Sam replied.

"Westfield. Her husband worked with Dad. We need to have a meeting with him so we can ask him about Curtis. We're at the point now where we definitely need some help."

"Good idea," Sam said.

Nim was frowning. "I think you guys are making a big mistake," she said.

"I'm with Paul," Sam said. "I say we go talk to the doctor's husband."

"Two against one. It's decided. We'll do it," I said. I rummaged through my pocket for the piece of paper with the phone number on it.

Nim held up her hand. "Don't, Paul!"

Sam snatched the piece of paper from my hand. "I'll call him," he said in a disgusted voice, and he ran off into his room. Nim gave me a worried look.

Sam returned a few minutes later with triumph on his face. "He said he has to come to Bayview today, anyway, to check up on their summer house. He's going to meet us at two o'clock at Grounds for Peace. He said the coffee's on him."

"Good," I replied.

"You don't drink coffee," Nim said. "Which is why I'm going with you."

30

David Westfield was a tall man with a broad face and a large head that appeared to be even bigger because he was bald on top. He had a gray, well-trimmed beard that looked dignified. He had on a pair of dressy blue jeans that suited him okay—not like he was trying to pretend to be younger than he was. His fancy shirt was made out of some kind of no-wrinkle fabric and looked comfortable on him. He had the air of a person who gathered no wrinkles and shed all dirt. His smile was friendly, and his eyes sparkled, a deep blue, behind his wire-rimmed glasses.

I found myself liking and trusting him right away, but I reminded myself to remain cautious.

We carried our drinks to a table by a window and sat down.

"Well, Paul," David said, "there seems to be something troubling you." His eyes had an open, innocent expression.

Sam kept staring at David's eyelashes, which were very long and curled slightly.

"And I assume it has to do with your father's tragic disappearance," David added.

I nodded. I wasn't sure how to begin.

"I wish I could help you. Your dad was a wonderful scientist—brilliant beyond description—and a true friend. But as far as what happened to him, I'm as stymied as the rest of the scientific community."

"There's been a rumor about what happened to him," Sam muttered with a frown. "A bad rumor."

"Well, it's never good to believe rumors, is it?" David replied.

"That's true," I agreed. I appreciated how reasonable he was.

"I can't help you find your father. But if there's something else, perhaps, where I might be of service . . ."

"There certainly is," Sam broke in again. "It's that rat Curtis."

"Curtis?" David asked. His eyes widened, and he turned to me with a questioning look.

"We've been worried about Curtis," I told him.

David's large head nodded. "Curtis is a puzzle," he replied. "Has he been coming into your life at all?"

I explained that our mother had invited him over recently—that in fact, Curtis was there when the truck sideswiped Mom.

David's thin eyebrows rose at the news. "Really?" he commented. "He was there at the time of the accident?"

"Yes," Sam told him. "Right there. Right there with her, but *he* didn't get hit by the truck."

Nim stirred in her seat.

David nodded slowly and made a motion with his mouth.

"Does that seem significant in some way?" Nim asked him.

"Oh no," David said. "Not really. Except . . ."

He paused. He seemed uncertain about how much he should tell us.

31

"Except what?" I asked. Beside me, Sam was disappearing behind a huge hot chocolate with whipped cream on top.

"Well, I don't mean to say anything negative about a colleague. But for some reason, trouble always seems to follow Curtis."

"What sort of trouble?" Nim asked.

He pursed his mouth. "Curtis is a strange fellow . . . difficult to understand. Quite brilliant, mind you. An excellent scientist. And a competent lecturer. Yet there always seem to be questions of one sort or another around him. Nothing I can really discuss with you. But I would be concerned if he's ended up on your doorstep once or twice too often."

"Once was already one time too many," Sam put in, "as far as I'm concerned." He turned his attention back to his hot chocolate.

With Sam's comment, the conversation reached a temporary lull. For the next few minutes, we talked generally about the difficulties of moving forward after a tragedy in the family. "Your father was so highly respected," David said. He shook his head sadly. "I hope to God he can be found. A true gentleman, and a pioneer in a very important field."

"Nanotechnology," Sam offered, proud to show off his knowledge.

"Are you aware of some of the amazing promise of this new area?" David asked.

"Oh yeah," Sam said. "I mean, for them to walk around and talk . . ." he stopped suddenly.

Nim and I glared at him.

"Sam's talking about the animated cartoon stuff their father used to make for them on his laptop," Nim interjected.

"Yeah, the talking carrots," I added. "They were so cool."

"Yeah, right, the carrots," Nim agreed.

Sam stared in silence at his hot chocolate.

David's blue eyes sparkled. "He had remarkable talents." He smiled sadly and glanced at his watch. "Well, I hate to say it, but I have to get to another meeting. I fear I've been of no help to you."

"You've been a real help," I said. "Um . . . could we call you again if we have any problems with Curtis?"

"Of course," David said. "Anytime. Do you have my cell phone?" He gave us the number.

"Thanks," we said.

"You don't fear for your safety, do you?" David asked.

"Should we?" Sam asked.

"No. No, I really don't think so. Curtis is eccentric, but . . . no, I wouldn't go that far. Unless . . ."

"Unless what?" Nim asked. She was watching David very closely.

"Well, he's been doing some very advanced work in nanotechnology himself, and there have been some concerns in high places about its safety."

"How would we know if it wasn't safe?" Nim asked.

"Just . . . just be careful. If you see anything really unusual, let me know."

"We will," Nim promised, giving Sam a look that warned him to keep quiet. "We will."

We shook hands with him and said good-bye, and he strode out of the coffee shop and disappeared down Broad Street.

"No, we haven't seen anything unusual," I said. "Just psychopathic flying scissors."

"We should have told him," Sam said. "I was going to, but you looked like you would bite my head off."

"You already *had* told him," Nim replied.

"He didn't know what I meant," Sam retorted.

"Like heck he didn't."

I tossed my cup into the trashcan by the exit. "I can tell he has real doubts about Curtis," I said. "But he didn't want to come right out and say what they were."

"Maybe so," Nim said. "Maybe so." She finished off her mocha, stood up, and tossed her paper cup after mine.

"Whoa . . . what's this?" Sam exclaimed as we stepped outside.

32

Curtis was standing right in the middle of the brick sidewalk. He was scowling and holding up a hand for us to stop.

"What's going on, Curtis?" I asked.

"Were you meeting with that man?" Curtis asked.

Sam and I glanced at each other. I shook my head: *Don't answer.*

"Yes," Nim told him. Sam and I glared at her.

"I hope you didn't tell him anything."

"What was there to tell him?" Sam asked, in his sing-song, I'm-an-innocent-little-boy voice.

"Do you have any idea how dangerous that man is?" Curtis asked. His pale blue eyes seemed to bore right into our souls.

"He seemed nice enough," I came back. "He was a friend of Dad's."

Curtis snorted. "You need to be very careful what you tell him," he said.

"How do you know we told him anything?" I challenged him.

"You know as well as I do that there are some things that can't be discussed right now." He looked at me with burning eyes.

Nim turned to Curtis. "If you're trying to say that you know something we don't, we'll be glad to talk to you anytime."

"First I have to try to undo the damage you've done," he grunted, then turned and loped off down the street after David Westfield.

"He looks like a hyena when he walks," Sam said. He imitated Curtis's strange sidelong motion.

"Pretty isn't always good," Nim said.

"Ugly isn't either," Sam came back. "What was he doing here, anyway?"

"He was tracking us," I muttered. "The weasel."

"Someday you'll be glad he's your friend," Nim said.

"Yeah, when hell freezes over," Sam replied.

"Stranger things have happened," she asserted.

Making his way down Main Street, Curtis shrank into a tiny dark point and then vanished—like a subatomic particle slipping through the fragile membrane that separates one universe from another.

33

"We need some fun in our lives," Sam declared that night, after we had fed Mom dinner and helped her go back to bed. "I mean, we're kids, aren't we?"

"Last time I checked," I replied. I clicked away at my keyboard—I was sending out personal appeals about Dad to scientists at various universities around the nation.

"What kind of fun?" Nim asked. She had been having a bit of fun of her own, helping some of the Hearts and Spades children put on a drama based on *Romeo and Juliet.*

Sam shook his head and snorted. "What about Holi? We didn't celebrate Holi this spring. We never missed it before. Every year at MIT, out in the square."

Nim looked up and asked, "What's Holi? I've heard about it but I don't really get it."

Sam tried to explain. Holi is a Hindu celebration of early spring that began in India and Nepal. It's a time for fun and color—and sweet pranks. The basic idea is to smear each other with bright colors from bags of powder known as *gulal.*

"It's too late in the year for Holi," I told Sam.

"I know," he muttered.

I glanced over at his computer screen. He had one of his Temptations videos playing. The great soul group of the '60s was singing—and dancing—one of their big hits: "Ain't Too Proud to Beg." Nim followed my eyes, saw the video, and turned toward Sam.

"Why don't you teach the card people the Temptations' dance moves?" she suggested to him.

Sam nodded and pursed his lips. "That's not a bad idea," he mumbled. Soon afterwards he called over Jack and some of the Diamond children, and he started putting them through their paces. It was the strangest dance class I've ever seen: the human child towering over the little card people, all of them executing, in synch, the identical spin moves and hand claps. It was like a bear cub dancing with a troop of crickets. All the while, Sam called out his directions: "Spin move, elbows forward, elbows back, raise hands, snap, step, repeat . . . Cross left . . . cross right . . . punch." His skin glowed with sweat.

Ridiculous? Yes. Crazy? Probably. But at least he was finally having some fun.

34

On Monday morning Sam and I said goodbye to Mom, who was staying home on sick leave, and I reported to the assistant principal's office for the second day of my internal suspension.

For the first half hour I was too distracted to do much work. There was a lot to think about. Mom and her recovery. The guys in the truck. The messages from the HOBO. Dad.

Finally I took out my big old math textbook and opened it up to the lesson of the day.

I was in the middle of copying out some problems when I heard Mr. Condor talking loudly in the hall.

"Well, not really, regulations don't really allow this type of suspension to be appealed, Mrs. Gibson," he was stating, in a very official voice. There was a murmur of voices arguing with him. "What's that?" he replied. "You've already obtained the permission of the School Committee?"

The upshot of it all was that a tall dark-haired boy and a short, round blond boy, wearing big smirks on their faces, were escorted into school a few minutes later in the direction of their first-period classes. A day early, Butch and Ken were back, by special order of the School Committee.

"What happened?" I asked Mr. Condor when he came back into the room.

He shook his head. "Butch's parents are good friends with the president of the School Committee, and they wanted their son back in school," he explained. "In the world of adults, sometimes it's not what's right, it's who you know." He shrugged.

Midway through the morning, I heard the pounding of feet outside in the hall and the clamor of excited voices, then more running feet, then someone screaming in the distance, and then Nim stood in the doorway, waving her arms.

"Paul, you've got to get to math class!" she yelled. "Hurry!" She turned and wheeled off down the corridor. I stumbled to my feet and ran after her, tucking the math book under my arm.

"What's going on?" I yelled after her.

"The scissors people!" she called back.

A shudder flickered through me.

When we came to Mr. Ellsbury's room, there was no teacher anywhere, and most of the kids were huddled in the back of the classroom.

In the front row, Butch sat alone at a desk, holding his left hand and crying. Maybe because of his attitude, Butch had always seemed much bigger than he really was. Now he looked small and terrified. There was a pool of very red blood on the desk in front of him.

Ken and the other kids were creeping around the back of the room towards the doorway, bent over like little kids playing hide and seek.

"There was a pair of scissors sitting on your desk when we came in," Nim explained. She took a few quick breaths. "When Butch picked them up, they . . . they began to cut him. At first everyone thought it was just a joke . . . till he started screaming and dropped them."

One of the guards, I realized. "Where are the scissors now?" I asked quietly.

She nodded. "On the floor next to him."

I glanced around the room. "Fill up the sink in the back of the room." While Nim scurried over to the sink, I eased over to Butch. My hands were shaking. *Take deep breaths*, I told myself.

If the scissors people could show up here, they could go anywhere now. A new level of hostilities had begun.

Butch looked up, terrified, like he was about to scream.

"Let's not disturb them." I nodded toward the scissors.

"Get 'em away from me!" he whined.

Without thinking, I knew how I needed to talk. Like a hero in an old action flick. Like one of the original ghostbusters. "Yeah, it's a weird thing, but some of the scissors these days are getting a little grumpy," I told Butch, with a little wave of my hand. "Probably don't like the taste of all that recycled paper. Let's see what we can do with this little guy." I hoped I didn't look as scared as I felt.

The pair of scissors on the floor seemed to sense that I was coming. Maybe it could smell me. It stirred on the linoleum tile . . . stood up, and took one clanky step forward. The black, expressionless eyes slid from side to side in the handles and then locked in on me.

An instant later the scissors were poised in front of me in the air, in full attack mode, with the sharp point aimed right at my chest.

I heard Nim draw in her breath in terror. Then she screamed.

There was no time to think.

It was all reflexes. The scissors shot straight at me like an arrow, and I threw up the math textbook like a shield. The impact flung me backwards over a desk, and I landed on the floor, smashing into another desk. I sat up. I was alive. The math book was still in my hands. The scissors had embedded their point deep into the book. They squirmed . . . but they were stuck.

As Nim rushed up to me, I rolled back onto my feet and lifted the book carefully in front of me. I carried it over to the sink and dunked it—with the scissors still stuck in it—into the pool of water. Book and scissors fell to the bottom of the sink and were still.

"Will that do it?" Nim asked, peering over the edge of the sink.

"I don't know."

"I thought it took salty water to kill them."

"Never underestimate the power of a math textbook."

The other children looked from Nim to me and then, led by Ken, they ran screaming in a group out of the room.

Butch climbed up to his feet, knocked over a desk, and shuffled out the door after them, clutching his wounded hand.

"Get that thing out of here!" he cried.

Nim and I bent over the sink. For now, at least, this pair of scissors was immobilized.

35

About an hour later, Mr. Condor met with the math class along with Mrs. Knockway, the school guidance counselor. Everyone except Butch was there. He'd gone to the hospital for stitches. Kelly took a look at Nim, flipped her hair, and turned away.

Mrs. Knockway was the tall woman who met with me a few weeks earlier. She smiled her toothy smile.

"Now children," she was saying, "there is a phenomenon known as mass hysteria. Everyone *believes* they have seen something that it was impossible for them to have seen."

"But Mrs. Knockway . . ." one of the girls tried to put in.

"No buts, young ladies. Let's remain perfectly rational about this. We all know that it is completely impossible for a pair of scissors to attack someone. The only logical explanation is that Butch was pulling a harmless prank . . . and then it went awry, it went out of control, and he hurt himself. It was nothing but an unfortunate accident."

"You may think that, Mrs. Knockway, but how do you explain the scissors in the math book?" Ken asked. For once his shark-like eyes had a real expression in them—fear.

"Well, Ken, it seems to me that Paul was having a little bit of fun at our expense," Mrs. Knockway said, with a knowing little smile. "Weren't you, Paul?"

I paused and looked at Nim, who nodded slightly, almost imperceptibly.

"Yes, Mrs. Knockway, I was," I admitted.

"What did you say, young man?" she asked. "You're mumbling."

"I said yes, that's right," I repeated, louder.

"You saw how hysterical and upset everyone was, and you just couldn't help playing to the crowd, could you, dear?" Mrs. Knockway prompted me, with a knowing little smile.

"That's exactly right, Mrs. K," I agreed. "Everyone was so scared . . . I fell on purpose over the desk. I don't think anyone saw me stab the math book with the scissors."

"No way!" one of the boys called out. "I saw the scissors with my own eyes! They were hanging there in the air! And then they flew at him like a bullet!"

"Me too!" some others cried. "I saw it too!"

I looked down at my hands.

"Those scissors went in so far, they probably even got to the chapter on geometry!" someone else exclaimed. Mrs. Knockway chuckled sympathetically. "There you have it, my dears. Mass hysteria. A textbook example." She glanced over at Mr. Condor and winked. He smiled back, a bit uneasily.

"What puzzles me is, these kids really seem to remember this," he said to her.

"Oh, no no no no no," she came back to him in a jolly way. "You know, recent research on memory has shown that we *create* virtually everything that goes into our memory banks. Some of it is accurate, but much of it is completely manufactured. When the fear part of the brain is activated—as it was today—there's no telling what our memory will conjure up. Attacking scissors indeed!"

"Then why do we all remember the same thing?" someone challenged her. "Did we all make it up at the same time?"

"Mass hysteria," she chuckled. "Mass hysteria."

36

I guess Mr. Condor decided to forget about my in-school suspension, because I spent the rest of the school day in my usual classes.

Nim and I kept texting each other secretly during the day, discussing our next moves. We figured that tap water might not be strong enough to disable those scissors for good. To be sure, we had to dump them into the bay.

After school let out, we found a plastic bucket in one of the custodians' closets, filled it full of water, and lifted the math textbook/scissors combo carefully into it. Little air bubbles formed along the raised letters of the MATH YOUR WAY title; one eye winked open in the scissors but then faded from sight.

By now, it was sort of a habit for Nim and me to leave school together.

"They all think you're really brave," she commented as we left the campus.

"I was lucky."

"No one believes it was mass hysteria," she remarked. The sun came out from behind a cloud, and she squinted and held her hand to her eyes, watching a snowy egret soar over the rooftops.

"Well, you were right. It's better if they don't really know what's going on," I observed.

We tried to figure out why the scissors had attacked Butch. Nim's theory was that the scissors could sense that Butch had held the cards recently . . . and then when I showed up, they recognized their real target.

The town pier was a huge wooden dock. At the end of it, large commercial fishing boats tied up between voyages. The timber was old and cracked and smelled of tar pine. A number of smaller mini-docks branched off at right angles like limbs on a tree. We walked partway out on one of them. A school of fish drifted lazily in the green water.

"Here we go." I lowered the pail into the water and tipped it. The book and scissors, still locked together, tumbled away into the murky depths.

"Bye bye," Nim told them.

"Rust in peace," I added.

"And good luck with factoring quadratic equations," Nim said.

We headed back toward shore.

"Sam's boat is over there," I said. "Have you ever seen it?"

"No, but I'd like to."

We stepped off the dock and continued down the shoreline. The beach grass looked drab and spindly in the afternoon glare. No shadows, just a dull light that made everything look sort of lonely. We came to the rack.

"His is the one with the green hull," I said.

"Oh, what a pretty little boat!" Nim exclaimed. She leaned in closer. She gave a little cry. "Oh no."

"What's wrong?"

"Look at this, Paul!" She pointed to the hull. Six little holes had been drilled into its bottom—three on each side, one inch in diameter, very neat.

"What the heck!" I exclaimed.

"Who would do such a thing?" she asked.

"I think I might have an idea," I replied.

"Could the scissors have done it?" she asked.

"Maybe. But more likely a crazy guy with a ballpoint pen and a drill."

A frown pinched her brow. "You have no reason to think this was Curtis."

"I don't trust him, Nim."

She stood up and glanced about. "Well, whether it's Curtis or someone else, we have to be really cautious from now on," she said.

I glanced around. There was something creepy about the still, shadowless light. "That's for sure," I replied.

If the scissors people were already able to launch an attack in my school in broad daylight, what was waiting for us at home?

37

For the moment at least, home looked and felt as safe as always—our comfortable old Victorian house, with its clapboard siding in need of paint and its cool round tower with the onion dome on top. There was even some good news: Mom was up, and she felt good enough to cook dinner.

Brinda raised herself onto her feet, nuzzled our hands, trotted out into the back yard to pee, and joined us in my room.

"It seems like she's having fewer 'accidents' these days," Nim observed.

"Yeah," I replied. "And that's really good news, because no one's talking now about how we can't keep her anymore."

"I think her friendship with the card people is making her feel younger and friskier." Nim watched as Brinda ran about and sniffed at the Queens, wagging her tail. They petted her and cooed over her.

The Aces fluttered about the room for a few seconds and flew out the window and were gone. Some of the Club children had wrapped themselves in thread and were practicing their kite moves by the open window. The face cards were huddled together on the desk, talking earnestly.

Sam knocked on the door and came in. He had already heard about the attack at school, and now he listened in silence as I broke the news to him about his boat. "It was Curtis," he said. "It had to be him."

"It could have been the scissors," Nim repeated.

"We need to talk to that other guy again. You know, David," Sam went on. He had a ridiculous expression in his eyes that he gets sometimes—total certainty that he was right.

"Not so fast," Nim cautioned.

"Nim, it's so obvious," Sam came back.

After the meeting of the face cards broke up, Jack hopped down from the desk and skittered along the floor to where we sat.

"I have some unfortunate news from the Aces, I'm afraid." He cleared his throat. His tiny face wore a grim expression. "The scissors people have already begun to recover. They have been hooked up again to their power generator, and we are in grave danger of an attack in the next few days."

"Oh, man, not already!" Sam shook his head.

We all exchanged looks. "What can we do?" I asked.

"We have little choice but to launch another offensive— with the goal of disabling them again. The Aces are out and about, gathering information even as we speak," Jack revealed.

"We can't attack them. We have no boat," Sam reminded him.

Jack tilted his little head to the side.

"If the weather favors us . . . that is, if the wind is from any direction but the north . . . we can make use of our new wind technology."

Sam shook his head. "You can't ride a scooter across the water."

"There may be other ways." Jack invited Nim to come with him, and they talked awhile in private.

After Nim left, I called David Westfield. He was very friendly and asked how things were going. I told him about the boat and said we suspected Curtis. David didn't say much in response, but he sounded worried.

"Could we meet again?" I asked.

"This evening's bad for me," he replied. "But tomorrow afternoon . . . say two-thirty? Are you finished with school by then?"

"Yes, we can be there."

"Listen," David warned, "be very vigilant. Try not to let him in your house at all, if you can help it."

It was good to have David on our side. At least we weren't alone anymore. Later, Sam and I talked about whether or not we should tell David about the card people. Sam was definitely in favor of it, but I still wasn't sure.

Late that afternoon, I logged into my emails and found another message.

> Subject: Something to Remember.
> When you shut out others, you weaken yourself.
> Be an open page, not a book on a shelf.
> —HOBO

When would all this end?

38

Just after sunset, a full moon floated free of the eastern horizon, pale and orange, like a hot-air balloon. It seemed to hesitate there for a few minutes and then lifted itself over the gray hills on the far side of the bay.

Brinda trotted along beside us as we made our way down to the shoreline. Mom was exhausted after cooking dinner, and had fallen into a sound sleep in her bed.

In the dusky darkness, a river of silver moonlight poured across the bay. Boats turned lazily on their lines. The breeze smelled of wild roses and honeysuckle, citrus and sweet.

As we approached the boat rack, a dark shape separated itself from the shadows. Brinda tensed and growled, but relaxed as Nim slipped forward and merged with this new shadow.

"You got it?" she asked.

"Got it," Lex replied, bending close to hand her something.

"What's this called again?" she asked. Again her voice had those new, breathy undertones.

"The Treefruit Wooden Kazoo. Best kazoo on the market—and unparalleled as a boat for a card traveler. Retrofitted with corks in the ends. Completely waterproof and buoyant."

"Oh, I get it," Sam announced. "A water scooter." He bumped fists with Lex. "How are you, bro?" Sam asked, trying to act like a cool high schooler.

"Ah . . . a little nervous," Lex admitted, bending down toward Sam. "Card people freak me out a little."

When we reached the shoreline, the cards got to work, playing out some thread and wrapping themselves in it. The Queen of Clubs, with the help of the Jack of Clubs, was tying off one end of the thread to the top of the "boat." The King and some of the children had lashed a metal bar to its side.

In a few minutes they were ready.

The card people waited on the sand, bound to one another by strands of slender thread, while the Queen of Clubs stood apart beside her boat. At the next wind gust, the Jack of Clubs lifted an arm, and the cards jumped into the air, straining against the thread as the wind caught them. Around them flitted the three Aces, who had returned to guide them on their journey.

"Prepare to launch!" the Queen called. She lifted up her anchor (a lead fishing weight), hopped onto the platform, and seated herself. She placed her steering oar (a stirring stick from the coffee shop) in the water beside her.

"Launch!" she called.

And away they went. Pulled by the card people kite, the boat bubbled off through the water, leaving a thin dark wake. Somewhere in the distance, a gull cried.

We waited in silence on the cool sand. Brinda climbed up onto Sam's lap. Lex put his arm around Nim, and she rested her head on his shoulder. Something tumbled in my stomach like a wet load of laundry.

In an hour or so they returned, silently and swiftly. The tiny boat seemed to lift free of the water as it approached the land. Seated on her little platform, the Queen of Clubs brought the boat in to shore and, with her steering oar, turned the hull sideways, so that it washed gently up onto the sand, bringing a few tiny waves with it. The cards dropped to the sand. They chattered happily, untying the thread and packing it away.

Soon Jack was perched on my shoulder.

"Success?" I asked.

"Success," he confirmed.

"I don't get what you did," Sam complained.

As the others gathered around, Jack explained it all. They had landed on the shore and moved in secret to the new, deeper hideout of the scissors people. There they carried out their new plan.

"Recently the children discovered, if we all hold hands, we can create a significant electrical current. As you may know, such a current, placed around a core of iron, creates magnetic force. With the Aces generating a large additional voltage, we were able to create a force of overwhelming magnitude."

"So basically, you stuck the scissors people together?" Sam asked.

"Yes. This generation of scissors people has been disabled for good . . . or so we hope," Jack replied.

There were cheers all around.

"Wait a minute," Sam said. "Am I the only one around here with a brain?"

Jack tilted his head and looked toward Sam.

"Sure, you created a magnetic force . . . but didn't it go away as soon as you left?" Sam asked.

Nim shook her head. "Don't fifth graders learn about inducing magnetism?" she said.

"I don't know, maybe," he replied.

"Too many homework assignments that you blew off," I commented.

Nim wagged a finger at Sam. "Have you ever seen a screwdriver that picks up screws on its own?"

"Yeah, so what?"

"Well, things that are made of magnetic material will *become* magnets themselves if they're exposed to magnetic force. I expect that's what happened to the scissors people."

"That is correct," Jack acknowledged. "The scissors people immediately became super-magnetized. We left them completely immobilized."

"For how long?" Sam asked.

"That's a good question. We're not sure," Jack admitted.

Lex picked up his kazoo and was about to stuff it into his pocket, but Nim put her hand on his.

"Can I carry it?" she asked.

"Sure, if you really want it." He handed her the kazoo.

"Thanks, I do," she said, giving him a quick kiss on the cheek. Their shadows merged.

Sam gave me a look of disgust, and we walked home.

39

Early the next morning, the card people began work on a new project—an electric car made out of cardboard, using an axle and wheels from a toy car.

The vehicle was soon ready for its test. Four Club children hopped onto the platform and joined hands in a circle. The Ten of Clubs took his place on the front and grabbed hold of a lever. His good-natured face, composed of ones and zeros, squinted with determination.

"Card children, start your engines!" the Jack of Clubs called.

There was a brief moment when nothing seemed to be happening. Then the tiny car commenced rolling slowly and silently across my room, gathering speed as it went. Sam and I cheered. I pulled open the door, and the car shot out into the hall—right through Brinda's legs.

Brinda turned and gave chase down the hall, but the Ten of Clubs brought the vehicle around in a tight circle, ran back through her legs, and sped back down the hall toward us. His face looked like one gleeful smile. We humans stepped aside as the car zoomed back into the room. It was moving at top speed now, with no apparent way to slow down. Soon it bumped into a chair leg, lurched against the bedspread, and tipped over onto its side at the end of the room, sliding to a stop against the radiator. The card children hopped off and cheered, pounding their fists in the air.

There was a loud knock on the door. "What's going on in there, boys?" Mom asked.

"Nothing!" we called. I scurried to pick up the cards, and Sam hid the car under the bed. "Nothing at all!"

She opened the door and peered in, frowning.

At school later that morning, I was back in class for every period, as usual. But it felt kind of different. The other students kept their distance. Everyone, including Ken and Butch, gave me space. It might have been respect, it might have been fear, it might have been distrust or dislike. I wasn't sure, and for once I didn't care. My thoughts were in other places, mostly on the meeting we'd scheduled for later that afternoon with Westfield.

At the end of the day, Butch ran up to me.

"How you doing, Kapadia?" he asked.

"Good," I said.

"Yeah, well that's all right."

He bumped his bandaged fist against mine and walked off. It came as a complete surprise, and it felt pretty darn good.

40

On the way to the meeting with David Westfield, I made a quick stop at the house to check on Mom, then went outside to wait for Sam by the driveway. It was another empty, lonely afternoon. A mud puddle swirled in the chilly breeze. Spring is never as great as people expect it to be.

There was a tiny crunch of gravel, and a red Prius pulled in the driveway.

I wondered what Curtis was up to.

And there it was, on the front passenger seat. No need for further doubt—it was in plain sight—a portable electric drill, with a wide bit that would fit perfectly into the holes that had been drilled in Sam's boat.

The last piece of evidence had fallen into place.

Curtis opened the door and stood up.

"Hi, Sam. Your mother asked me to come over," he said. As usual, his face showed no emotion of any kind.

"I'm Paul, not Sam."

"I'm sorry, Paul, I knew that." He looked toward me blankly. "Is something wrong?"

"Is that your drill?" I asked.

"No, it's from the lab."

"What's it doing in your car?"

"Why should I need to answer that?" Normally, an adult would ask that question in a scornful way, but Curtis seemed genuinely curious.

"Because I need to know," I replied.

Curtis stared at me for a moment, his eyes growing darker.

"Well, I found it in the lab this morning, and I remembered that I need to drill a hole in my kitchen baseboard to run some wires down to the basement. Is something wrong?"

"Drilling holes in your house is fine. Drilling holes in Sam's boat is not."

Curtis looked puzzled. "What are you talking about, Paul? Why would I drill holes in Sam's boat?"

"You take one step closer to the house, and I'm calling the police," I warned him.

"Paul, I'm only here to make sure you all are safe."

"Oh yeah, I like that. To make sure we're safe."

Curtis was looking directly at me. He showed no trace of hostility. His blue eyes were squinched up in confusion. "Did I do something that offended you?"

"Oh, no, nothing," I came back sarcastically.

"Good. Well, then, may I come in?"

"Sure . . . if you want me to call the police."

Curtis took a step back. "Paul, am I to understand that you aren't joking? Do you really intend to call the police?" he asked.

"Just try me."

He shrugged. "All right then, I guess you're on your own."

"Good. That's how we want it."

He got into the car and started it up. The utter silence of the hybrid seemed eerie, almost evil. He backed out of the driveway and glided away into the late April afternoon.

When Sam showed up a minute later, bopping along down the street happily, I told him about the drill.

He pounded his right fist into his left hand. "I knew Curtis was a rat. So we *can* trust David!"

I nodded. "Yep. Nim had it wrong this whole time."

41

By 2:30, we were seated at one of the little round tables in Grounds for Peace. I tapped the cards in my shirt pocket. Sam looked around the room anxiously.

"Smile. Be relaxed," I told him.

"You're not one to talk, bro. You're sweating like a pig."

A few minutes later, David Westfield strode into the coffee place. No casual dress today—he was wearing a charcoal gray suit, with a red silk tie embossed with blue diamonds. His eyebrows were pulled together in an expression of concentration. He looked handsome and self-possessed and businesslike.

He smiled when he saw us. "The usual?" he asked.

"The usual," we replied.

David nodded and went up to the counter to order.

A few minutes later he joined us at the table and passed out the drinks. "Where's your friend?" he asked.

"Nim?" I replied. "She couldn't make it."

He nodded. "So, how are we doing?"

"Not so great," Sam replied.

"More problems with a certain person?" David inquired.

"Yes." I took a sip of my mocha and set it down.

"Anything in particular?" David asked. His wide, intelligent face seemed to radiate interest and helpfulness.

"Well, he keeps coming into our house," Sam complained. "We think he tried to destroy our . . . well, some important things that we have."

"What sorts of things?" David asked, casually.

"Some cards and stuff," Sam replied. I gave him a look.

"I told you about our boat," I said. "And now we're beginning to wonder if he was involved somehow in Mom's accident."

"You think that was planned?" David asked. "You think that someone was *trying* to harm your mother?"

"Does that sound crazy?"

"Well, at first blush, it might. But, maybe not . . . if you knew Curtis as I know him." David smiled ruefully. His eyes made contact with mine. I felt as if I'd been admitted into a special circle of people who were in the know. "He's very difficult to understand, and personally I don't trust him."

"He has no emotions," Sam remarked.

"You are very perceptive. That's exactly what the problem is," David agreed. Sam's face lit up at the compliment.

"You worked pretty closely with our dad, didn't you?" I asked.

"Oh yes. For many years—more than I'd like to remember. Your father was a brilliant scientist, and I was proud to call him a friend."

"Did you work on . . . nanotechnology?" Sam asked.

"Yes, of course," David answered, with a slight smile. "We made some extraordinary progress, and in fact, to speak quite candidly, we came very close to creating the first new life forms of the twenty-first century."

"You did?" Sam asked.

"We did."

"What stopped you?" I inquired.

"Well—to be candid—what he wanted to do was impossible."

"What did he want to do?" Sam asked.

"He wanted to create some sort of magic dust that would animate whatever it touched. You sprinkle it on a fork, and the fork comes to life, with the power to move, the power to speak. Or you sprinkle it on a teddy bear, and it cuddles up to you." David smiled disarmingly.

"Or on scissors," Sam said. "Then you would get mean scissors." I kicked him under the table.

David was watching us closely. "Scissors . . ." he said, letting the word draw out. "Scisssssssors. Has either of you seen any *scissors* that are alive?" he asked in a creepy voice. We stared at him. Then he smiled again, and the expression in his eyes was open and innocent. "Scissors that give you a haircut all by themselves? Scissors that cut up a piece of paper for you? Yeah, sure, I see them all the time." He laughed at his own joke. He stole a quick glance at both of us.

"Well, we haven't seen them," Sam replied. "Nope, no scissors."

"There's a good reason why your father couldn't accomplish this," David said. "And I don't want you boys to take this the wrong way."

I looked at him in silence.

"Take what the wrong way?" Sam asked. I could hear the beginnings of confusion, maybe anger, in my little brother's voice.

"What your father thought he could do . . . well, it can't be done. It turns out that it's impossible to create a new form of life."

Sam opened his mouth as if to refute him, and I gave Sam a look that shut him up.

David continued, "Those creatures—if he did in fact set them in motion—are actually quite dangerous. They can't learn or make rational decisions, like normal life forms. In fact, they have been programmed to hate all creatures that have emotions—just like Curtis. So, if such creatures do exist, they are highly dangerous, no matter how cute or sweet they may appear."

By now Sam had his stubborn, I'm-right-you're-wrong look in his eyes.

"Well, you're wrong," he declared.

David's blue eyes blinked innocently behind his glasses. "Wrong about what?" he asked.

"The card people. They're not dangerous," Sam blurted out.

"Sam!" I hissed.

David looked from Sam to me. "What card people?" he asked.

I shook my head. "My brother makes up things."

Sam gave me a little shove on the shoulder. "I do not, and you know it."

"Is there something you boys want to tell me?" David asked.

42

For a moment there was silence. Then Sam said, "We have them." He gave me a defiant look.

"You have what?" David asked.

It was too late to try to hide it any longer. Better to take a chance and hope for the best.

"We have the card people. And we know that Dad made them," I told David.

"Card people?" He tilted his head in a friendly way. "Tell me about them."

We explained what we knew about the card people—the family differences, their rank, the behaviors that they all shared, including their desire to help living things that are in trouble.

David listened carefully.

"Very, very interesting," he said. "But that last piece, about helping living creatures—that's all a ruse. Believe me, their intentions are not at all peaceful."

"How can you be sure?" I asked.

"I'd better give you some background. A quick primer on molecular chemistry." David launched into a discussion of valences and chemical bonds. His explanation was long and complex and difficult to follow. He watched our faces closely as he spoke. "So you see, nanotechnology as your father envisioned it is, in fact, simply not possible. Which means that these 'life forms' are not, in fact, what they seem. They can't learn. They can't make good decisions. They aren't, in fact, alive."

"What are they then?" Sam asked.

"Walking iPads. Robots. And quite unsafe."

"I can tell you really believe that," I said.

"May I see them?" David asked. His eyes glistened, and his tongue touched his lips.

"No," we both exclaimed, at the same time.

"No?" David asked. He sat back and smiled disarmingly. Again, I felt the comfort of that smile, the nice sense that we were all friends, that we should do as he wished.

"Not here," I added. "We have to keep them safe." Without thinking, I tapped my shirt pocket.

He blinked. "Of course. Maybe at the house sometime?"

"That would be better," Sam said. "That's a better place to see them." He was tapping me under the table—our prearranged signal. Sam wasn't sure he liked where this was going; he wanted to leave.

"Well, is there anything I can do for you before you go?" David asked. There was a slight change in his eyes, a hardening somewhere in the depths of his pupils.

I took the last sip of my mocha. "We were hoping you could give us some advice on how to deal with Curtis."

"Look," David said, "It's time I was straight with you. Curtis is a disturbed individual. He's obsessive compulsive. He's delusional. The best thing you can do is this: ask your mother to keep him away. By the way, I hope she's doing well."

"She's fine," I said.

"Tragic what happened to her," David clucked. "Just tragic."

We stood up, threw away our coffee cups, and stepped outside. We stopped and turned toward each other on the sidewalk to say our good-byes. Then David leaned forward. It looked as if he was about to shake hands with me, but instead—as casual and effortless as someone plucking an apple out of a basket—he snatched the deck of cards out of my pocket, took two quick scissor-steps to the side, and hopped into a Lexus that had pulled up alongside, driven by a young woman wearing large sunglasses.

43

"It's safer this way, boys," he called out the window, as the car tore off down the street and disappeared around the corner.

We ran after him, screaming to him to stop. We halted at the corner and looked at each other.

"What just happened?" I asked.

"He took the cards, Paul."

"I know that!" I seethed. "But why?"

Sam shook his head. "I don't know."

"Is he really trying to protect them?" I asked.

Sam shrugged. "We better hope so."

We talked for a few minutes, trying to understand. What was David intending to do? Did he want to keep the cards away from Curtis? Was he trying to keep us out of danger?

Or had he known along that we had something of great value . . . and had he played us for fools?

"It's gonna be okay," Sam said finally.

"Yeah," I agreed, without much enthusiasm.

We walked home in silence.

Spring was busting out everywhere around the town. Sticky red and yellow leaves were unfolding on the maples like little origami figures. The forsythia had burst out in armfuls of gold. Cherry blossoms drifted through the air.

But inside our hearts, the season had shriveled away into nothing.

When we came inside, Mom was sitting by the window, looking at a magazine. She had her half-size reading glasses on. "Hi, sweetie. What happened to Curtis?"

"He left," Sam grumbled. He stalked off to his room.

"He left?" Mom tried to find my eyes. "Is everything okay?"

"He forgot his pen. He went home to get it," I said.

Mom's brow wrinkled. "It's true, Curtis does have his little routines. It's because—"

"Mom, give me a minute, I need to check on something." I went up to my room to check my messages one more time.

I opened the laptop and logged on. And there it was, one more message.

> Subject: A Final Thought.
> Your father tried to rewrite the laws of creation.
> Death and destruction will descend on your nation.
> —HOBO

I sat there numbly, reading it over.

"Whatcha doing?" Mom stood in my doorway.

"Oh, hi, Mom." I quit the program, and the screen went blank.

"No need to stop what you were doing," she said. She sat down and leaned against my desk. She pulled a shawl around her shoulders. Her eyes looked tired, but they seemed clearer and more observant—more like Mom before the accident. "What a cute little house!" she exclaimed. "Did you make that?"

"Nim did."

"She did a great job, stairs, beds, doorways. She's very good."

"She is."

"It's the perfect size—for card people."

I turned and stared at her.

"Yes, I've known for a few days," she said. "Curtis and I finally figured it out."

Sam showed up in the doorway. "What are we talking about?" he asked.

Mom took a seat in my chair. "Boys, I need you to listen very carefully. There are some things I've got to tell you."

"Is this our 'talk?'" I asked.

"It is," Mom confirmed.

And so she finally told us about Dad.

44

For the past six or seven years, Dad had known that he had the ability to create a new breed of living creatures through nanotechnology. After years of work, he and a trusted co-worker had overcome every obstacle.

Shortly before his disappearance, with the help of tiny, intelligent nanorobots that he had created, he made the nanodust that was the apex of his work. It was able to "nanimate" whatever it touched, creating living beings with the ability to learn and with a built-in desire to help existing forms of life. That "helping" trait was crucial, because it ensured that humans and animals would not be harmed.

He had also designed a DNA lock, meaning the dust would only be activated in the right hands.

"His work was even more amazing because he accomplished it all despite the betrayal of someone else in the office— another associate," Mom continued.

About five years ago, that associate began to make some puzzling public pronouncements. He said that nanotechnology would turn out to be nothing more than a dream. He knew better, of course. It was all a ploy . . . but for what purpose?

Dad moved quietly forward with his work. He helped establish international standards for safeguards against replication—the ability of nano beings to create copies of themselves. And he intensified his own research.

Around this time there were some strange and troubling occurrences. Some of the sensitive equipment began to disappear from the lab. The associate was observed more than once talking to a pair of former CIA operatives who were rumored to be arms dealers—willing to sell anything to the highest bidder. There were signs that he needed large sums of money to fuel a new, fancier life style.

Dad feared that the associate was developing a deadly form of nanodust and might be creating a prototype for sale to an enemy of the US.

Not long after that, Dad became aware that someone was tailing him to and from work. Sometimes he saw an unmarked white van parked on the side streets outside his MIT office.

At that point he began to fear for his life, and he redoubled his efforts to complete the new version of the nanodust. He shared all his plans with the first co-worker—who was an expert on artificial intelligence—and made the co-worker promise to look out for his family if something happened to him. Though he had little free time now, he spent as much of it as he could with his children.

"He worried that he might not be here much longer. And you two were the most important people in the world to him," Mom said, and though her voice was still flat and expressionless from her accident, tears were trickling down her cheeks.

We came over and hugged her. For several minutes no one spoke.

45

"So Mom," I asked finally, "what happened to Dad?"

"That's the one thing I can't tell you," she replied. Her eyes glanced up toward me, then slid away.

"You can't . . . or you won't?"

"Paul, it isn't my choice."

"Then whose choice is it?"

"I'm not allowed to say."

"Mom, we've heard all the rumors. Is he alive?" I asked, steeling myself for the worst.

"I've told you everything I can."

I stood up in disgust, turned, and looked out the window. I leaned against the window frame and let my forehead rest against the cool glass.

"I'm sorry," Mom said softly. "One day you'll understand. And I hope you'll forgive me then."

"One day," I repeated. "One day."

Sam stood up and pounded his fist in his hand.

"Mom, we know who that rat is. And we know who the trustworthy co-worker is," he declared. I glanced up at him; I could tell that Sam was probably a step behind.

"It was Curtis!" Sam went on. "That's who it was!"

"*Who* was Curtis?" Mom asked.

"The rat."

I shook my head. "No," I said. "No, Sam."

Sam shot a confused glance my way.

"Curtis is the one you can trust," Mom replied. "The one who betrayed Dad is—"

"David Westfield," I finished, with a chill that ran down my spine.

Sam stared at me wide-eyed. "It was David?" he squeaked.

"David Westfield is a horribly dangerous man," Mom told them. "It's too bad that you met him. You must stay away from him at all costs."

"Too late," I replied.

"What do you mean?"

"Oh my God, I'm such an idiot!" Sam exclaimed, pounding his forehead.

"We were both idiots," I said. It was all becoming clear now. But there was one more question. "Mom, that house that sits all by itself on the Haul-over—is that David Westfield's?"

"Yes," she said. "It belongs to him and his wife—who is the doctor who cared for me at Mass General. A good doctor and a kind person, unlike her husband—who has gotten involved behind her back with one of his graduate students."

"Oh my God! Why didn't we see that earlier?" I exclaimed.

"See what?" she asked.

"No wonder the scissors people came from there!"

"Scissors people?" Her eyes widened.

Then, in a rush, I explained to her about the scissors people and all that had happened in the last few days. Sam sometimes added a sentence of explanation.

When we had finished recounting it all, Mom sat back and shook her head. "That's very bad news," she said. "It's gone much farther than I expected."

"There's something else, Mom," I said. I told her about Curtis—how we had misread him, how I had sent Curtis away that afternoon.

"That's understandable," Mom said. "He's hard to figure out if you don't know."

"Know what?" Sam asked.

She looked up. "Well, he has Asperger's syndrome. It's a form of autism. You may have heard of it."

"There's a kid at school who has it," Sam put in. "A couple of kids."

"Curtis doesn't really 'get' many human interactions," Mom explained. "They confuse him, and so he acts inappropriately. That's why people misinterpret him. Of course, your father thought his Asperger's might have helped him in his work."

She explained that Curtis's autism forced him to think in highly logical ways—with a kind of pure intelligence that non-autistic people could never hope to achieve.

"Sort of like Spock," Sam commented.

"In a way," Mom replied. "But Vulcans are fantasy, and Asperger's is for real. I'll call Curtis and invite him to come back, if that's okay with you."

"It's fine," I agreed.

"He's been very helpful. He came over and fixed my bicycle for me that afternoon because he thought Westfield had created something that could track my car—so a bike seemed like a safer way for me to get around."

Sam went over and gave her another hug. He could be a sweet kid sometimes.

"I wish we had figured out earlier that Curtis was a friend," I said. "But anyway, you'll need him here when we're gone."

She pulled away from Sam's hug and peered at me over her reading glasses. "Where are you going?"

"We've got to get the card people back."

Mom shook her head again. "No," she said. "Stay away from Westfield. He's too dangerous."

"Mom, we have no choice," I replied, and Sam nodded.

"I'm not going to lose my sons, too," she insisted, but I knew she couldn't stop us.

Over the past few years I had come to realize something about parents and children. There's a complicated system of give and take between them, and it's always shifting. At the moment, we held the advantage. When Mom made the decision to hold back the final information about what happened to Dad, it came at a price: It meant we could push forward on our own now, even against her wishes.

"Do you realize what will happen to us all if we don't get those cards back?" I told her.

Mom gazed at us in silence for a minute. She let out a sigh.

"You are your father's sons, and I love you," she said. "But tell Curtis to get the police to go with you." She leaned back on the chair. She looked, suddenly, very tired.

46

When the Prius pulled into the driveway, Sam and I filed out the door like a little greeting party. Curtis stepped out of the car, saw us, and froze.

"Hi, Curtis," I called.

"Hi," he replied. He watched in silence as we approached.

"Hey, I'm sorry about how I spoke to you the other day," I offered. "It's my bad."

"Yeah, we sort of got it all backwards," Sam admitted.

Curtis's eyebrows raised slightly, like little caterpillars waking up from a nap. "You were trying to protect your mother. That's the right thing to do," he said.

He didn't seem to resent how we'd treated him. As usual, he seemed free of any and all emotions.

"Yeah, my boat had these holes in it, and the drill was in your car, and so we thought . . ." Sam said.

"I suspect that David Westfield drilled the holes in your boat," Curtis stated.

"Yeah, that would make sense," Sam replied.

"Then, perhaps, he returned the drill to the lab, where I found it," Curtis continued.

"That makes sense, too," I said.

"Which lead to the unfortunate short-circuit in your process of reasoning," Curtis concluded.

"Uh, yeah. Sorry about that," I said.

"We can't help it if we're morons," Sam added.

"You aren't the first people to fall under the spell of David Westfield," Curtis observed. "For some reason he's never had that effect on me. Quite the opposite, in fact. I've never trusted him one bit." He jangled his keys and put them in his pocket. "Is your mother inside?"

"She's in the living room."

"What are your plans?" he asked.

"David Westfield has the card people," Sam told him. "Which—according to Mom—you know about now."

Curtis nodded.

"Well, we've got to get them back."

"But where are they?" Curtis asked. "And how will you get them back?" No doubt or disdain: just straightforward, direct questions.

"We know where his vacation house is," I said.

"What if he took the cards back to his place in Cambridge? Or to the lab at MIT? What if he burned them up already?" he asked.

"David destroyed my boat. He wouldn't have done that unless he wanted to keep us away from his vacation home," Sam reasoned.

"That's logical," Curtis commented.

On a sudden impulse, Sam raised his hand in the Vulcan salute, and Curtis matched him from across the drive. There was a faint glow, almost a smile, on his face.

"So how are you boys going to get there?" he asked.

"We have a way," I replied.

Curtis's eyebrows did another caterpillar dance. He bowed his head slightly and turned to go inside.

"Weren't we supposed to talk to him about getting the police to come with us?" Sam asked under his breath.

"No way we can do that, it would blow our cover," I replied.

47

A few minutes later, a rickety old Jeep Wagoneer came careen-
ing up the street and shuddered to a stop under the copper
beach tree at the end of our driveway. Nim hopped out of the
passenger side, saw us, and waved, all bubbly and happy. She
had grown even more like a bowling pin these past few weeks.

"Sweet! It's a woody!" Sam exclaimed. He ran his hand
along the wooden sides of the vehicle, and we climbed into
the back seat. Nim made sure we were settled comfortably and
then turned and met Lex's eye, giving a small nod of her head.
It looked like they could communicate now with nothing more
than little glances, like some old married couple. Something
crumpled inside me like wet cardboard.

"Thanks for driving us, Lex," I forced myself to say.

"No problemo," Lex replied.

"Is that your guitar in the back?" Sam asked.

"It's my beach guitar, my old one," Lex replied. He glanced
in the rear view mirror and pulled out onto the street.

"Exactly how far away are you from getting your license?"
Sam asked.

"About as far as anyone can be," Lex replied.

"How far is that?"

"In a year or so, I'll be eligible for a learner's permit."

"Awesome!" Sam exclaimed. "So how'd you learn to drive?"

Lex steered us smoothly around a curve. "A few years ago, my grandfather taught me on the back roads. He said everyone should know how to drive by age twelve. It might come in handy some day. So here we are."

"What about your dad?"

"Never met him. He split before I was born." Nim gave him a sympathetic glance. Lex drove carefully, glancing frequently into both mirrors, keeping two hands on the wheel. "Take a right up here?"

"Yep," I said.

"Everyone at school is pretty freaked out about those scissors," Nim said, turning briefly to me. "You're, like, a legend. No one believes for a second that you stabbed them all the way through that math book."

"It wouldn't hurt if a few more math books were put out of commission," Lex said in his serious/not serious way. Nim leaned closer to him and stroked his hair with her fingers. Sam looked at me, opened his mouth, and pointed a finger down his throat.

48

After about ten minutes, we pulled off onto a dirt road. Lex
stopped the car and got out to turn the hubcaps on the front
wheels to engage the four-wheel drive. Which is how it's done
in classic cars like the Woody, it seems. Then we drove on. The
road twisted along through shrub oak and bayberry bushes and
past a few small kettle ponds. Finally we reached the Haul-
over—the thin spit of land that separates the bay from the
ocean. Here the road became rutted and rough, and the old car
started to sway and buckle.

"Whoot! Whoot! Ride 'em cowboy!" Sam called.

"Quiet, Sam!" I told him. Didn't the kid know that some
things are serious?

To me it felt like being in a boat. Up, down, up, down. Over
the years, the beach traffic had cut a regular pattern into the
sand, almost like waves. I remembered that Dad once told me
that all roads, over time, are carved in the shape of a sine wave.
All motion tends toward a perfect curve, he said.

Nim bounced up and down, giving worried looks out the
window, whispering comments to Lex, and looking pretty perfect herself.

A shimmer of light through the beach plums meant we
were approaching the water. The road swung out onto the

beach. We glided over the smooth, hard sand at the high tide mark and then followed the tracks back into the rutted interior for the final approach.

Lex slowed down. "We're getting closer, and I'm going to come in as quiet as I can," he said.

Nim turned around in her seat.

"What's the agenda?" she asked.

"We have to snoop around first and figure out what's going on," Sam replied, with an air of authority.

"Sounds like a plan," Lex said, with no trace of sarcasm. He drove on. I had to admit, he seemed like a pretty good guy.

Lex stopped at the base of a low hill, pulling up as far as possible under a stand of scrub oaks.

We got out, pushed the doors quietly shut, and started in silence up the dirt road. Bayberry bushes and gnarly little pines were all that grew here—and poison ivy, tons of it, in shiny, three-leaf clusters.

After a few minutes a dark mass showed itself through the trees.

Nim stopped. "Is that it?" she whispered.

"That must be the roof," I whispered.

We crept closer.

"There are bushes next to the house. That'll give us some cover," Lex said, in a quiet voice.

Nim held up a hand to stop. "Seriously, Paul, what's the plan? Do you want us to come with you?" she asked.

"Sam and I will go first," I whispered back. "If you don't see us again after half an hour, we might need a little help."

"I should have brought my guitar so I could smash that guy over the head," Lex commented. He and Nim exchanged a look.

"Never fear," Sam assured them. "You will see us again in the wink of an eye, and we'll have our cool little friends with us."

Nim smiled. "That's the spirit!" She gave me a worried look.

The cottage sat on a low hill surrounded by a thin strip of weedy lawn. The front faced the water, and Sam and I were approaching from the rear.

We slipped from bush to bush and came to a window. We pressed closer and looked inside.

There was one large room with wood paneling on the walls and a lot of old wicker furniture, some of it covered with sheets. It looked completely deserted.

"Darn!" Sam exclaimed. "Where is he?"

"Maybe there's another section—like a basement or something," I said. "Let's check around front."

We made our way to the far corner.

"Look!" I pointed.

On this side of the house, a new addition had been built, complete with a basement that had been dug into the side of the hill. And beside it—separated by a wooden retaining wall—lay a driveway paved with scallop shells. The Lexus was parked there, gleaming in the soft April sun—and next to it, a dull red pickup truck.

"Those guys *are* working for David Westfield," I commented.

"Paul, this is getting weird," Sam muttered. His eyes were darting around, and his lips looked thin and nervous.

I tried not to let him see my legs shaking. "Let's take a look." I pointed at a basement window a few yards from us. A window well had been hollowed out beneath it, edged by a semicircle of metal. We wriggled forward on our stomachs until our chests hung out over the well, and pressed our faces up to the glass.

As our eyes adjusted to the light inside, I could make out the contours of a sleek, new laboratory. Somewhere inside, a motor rumbled—maybe a generator. A woman moved about the room, briskly and efficiently.

"Can you see the card people?" Sam asked. "I don't see them."

"Not yet," I replied.

"Oh, they're there, all right," said a smooth, familiar voice behind us. "Come have a look. Bring them inside, will you?" a male voice remarked casually.

At that, we were yanked roughly to our feet by the two guys from the truck.

49

None too gently, they dragged and shoved us around the side of the house.

"Hey, easy!" I protested, and got a quick blow to the stomach. The center of my body caved in, and I gasped for breath.

"Don't hit my brother, you jerk!" Sam exclaimed.

The guard gave him a glancing blow to the head and Sam starting crying. Up close these guys were crazy scary. Their eyes were glazed over and cruel, their noses were bent and flattened. They jerked us around to the entrance, opened the door and threw us down on the floor in the lab. There they stood over us, their massive arms crossed, looking with a bored expression toward the young woman who was working in the lab.

David Westfield appeared from an inside door.

"How are we doing?" he asked.

"I'm finally getting a reading," she replied.

"Excellent," he said, coming up beside her and resting a hand on her shoulder.

Sam tried to stand up, and one of the guards slammed him back down to the floor.

David Westfield wheeled in our direction.

"Sit still," he ordered. "This is a matter of national security. Do you realize the danger that you've placed our country in?"

"Liar, liar, pants on fire," Sam retorted. I gestured to him to be quiet.

I rolled up onto my knees for a better look. One of the cards—it looked like the Ten of Clubs—had been screwed down across a band of yellow metal, and electrodes had been attached to both ends.

David Westfield leaned in closer to a computer screen. "That's nothing but garbage coming out of him," he said.

"They're scrambling it on purpose. It's a default mode, probably a built-in security feature," the woman replied.

Westfield detached the electrodes, unscrewed the card, picked it up by a pair of tongs and carried over to the other side of the room. He started up a small blowtorch and raised it to the card.

"Anything you'd like to tell us now?" he asked.

The card did not respond.

Westfield touched the flame to the Ten of Clubs. It flared up in flames of green and gold and crumpled into a sad, gray ash.

"Maybe the next card will be a little more forthcoming," he commented.

"You're a murderer!" Sam called.

"Shut up!" Westfield ordered.

"You shut up! That card drove its first car this morning!"

One of the guards struck Sam across the face, harder this time. The blow knocked him over onto his side. When Sam sat up again, he had a red welt on his cheek, and a thin line of blood dripped out of his mouth. He was seriously sobbing now.

"Throw him a rag, Kristof," the woman commented. She was holding another card—the Queen of Spades—and screwing it down onto the strip of metal.

Stay calm, I told myself. I was thinking of our father. What would Dad do in a situation like this?

What was Dad's advice when you got in trouble?

You can always find your way to an answer. Don't let fear stop you. I cleared my throat and sat up. I knew I had to choose my words carefully.

50

"Don't listen to my little brother. He's young and he's stupid," I said. "I've been telling him all along how dangerous these cards are, but would he believe me?"

"Shut up, Paul!" Sam yelled.

"See what I mean?" I continued. "Some people have brains. He's not one of them."

"I think he's cute," the woman said. "I like his dark skin. Are you boys from the Philippines?" She shook back her long brown hair.

"Your butt wiggles when you move!" Sam snarled at her.

David Westfield raised an eyebrow toward the woman, and she smiled primly and kept working.

"Where are you keeping the other cards?" I asked casually.

"Oh, don't worry about them. They're each in their own little sleeve, so they can't cause any trouble," she replied. She fixed the electrodes in place.

"They don't struggle against you?" I asked.

"They can't. We froze them in a magnetic field."

"You boys have been playing with fire," Westfield commented. "Do you realize that each of these cards has more destructive power than a small nuclear weapon?"

"I've always been afraid of them," I explained. "That's why we came to you. That's why I told you about them when we met yesterday."

"Uh huh. And why did you come here today?"

"We got some new information about Curtis, and we wanted to see if we could do anything else to help." I spread my hands apart. "I think this is all a big misunderstanding."

"Right. You were so interested in trying to help that we caught you sneaking around back," Westfield replied.

"We had to make sure it was you. We were afraid Curtis might have already gotten here."

"He doesn't stand a chance against us," Westfield sneered.

"Look, there's one thing I just don't get," I said, lifting my hands innocently. "I don't understand why you took the cards from us. We would gladly have given them to you if you had asked."

Westfield smiled grimly. "Very gladly, I'm sure," he said.

"We're just kids. We want to help any way we can."

"More scrambled messages," the woman announced.

"Some like it hot," Westfield commented. He unscrewed the Queen of Spades, picked her up with the tongs, carried her across the room, and put the torch to her. In the midst of the orange, writhing flames I caught an image of the Queen for a split second, arms and legs extended, screaming in agony.

"You murderer," Sam muttered. "You disgusting piece of..." He got another smack on the face for his trouble.

"Don't be a jerk, Sam," I said.

"You're the jerk!" Sam cried. "I can't believe you! You're selling out!"

Westfield smiled. "Isn't brotherly love a wonderful thing?"

"May I ask you a question?" I inquired.

Westfield nodded.

"I know you want the card people to cooperate. Well, I have an idea. They might listen to me," I said. "Would you like me to speak to them?"

Westfield frowned. "Possibly."

"Maybe if I could explain to them what you're trying to get from them?"

"I'm trying to get their code, of course," he replied, in an off-hand way. "We need to see just how diff . . . just how dangerous it is."

"If I tell them to trust you, they might cooperate. I mean, hey, if someone froze me and stuck electrodes on me, I might not be real helpful either."

Sam was still scowling at me. But there was a different look in his eyes now. He was starting to understand what I was trying to do.

For a few moments Westfield was silent.

"You're making the mistake of assuming that they have free will," he said. "But it won't hurt to try, I suppose. Julie?" he prompted.

Julie was holding the Jack of Hearts in her tongs.

"Set him down on the table," David told her. "Let him go free a moment. I've got the stun gun if there's any trouble."

Julie placed the card on the table.

For a minute nothing happened, but then Jack unfolded himself into his card person form and stood up. He remained in one spot, rigid and silent.

"What a cute little face," Julie exclaimed, "and a such truly round little head!"

"May I stand up?" I asked. Westfield nodded.

I came over closer. "Jack?" I asked. "Jack? Can you hear me?"

There was no motion at all. He seemed to be frozen in place.

51

I tried again.

"Jack, it's me, Paul. We're in a safe place. Try to focus now. We need to talk."

Jack took a stiff step forward and stopped.

"How are you feeling?" I asked him.

He took another step forward, then back. His motions were very stiff and clumsy.

"How are you feeling?" I asked again, emphasizing each word.

Jack turned and looked at me. He bent his arms, swayed them stiffly forward and back—like an exaggerated version of a move from the Temptations—and rested them again at his side.

"Who are you?" Jack asked, in a dull, robotic voice.

"What do you mean, who am I? I'm Paul."

Jack stared at me. "Data inputs indicate an unknown entity, a carbon-based life form of uncertain origin."

"Jack! We've been playing with each other for, like, a week or two now."

Jack turned to David Westfield. "This life form is unknown to me. My heat sensors are detecting hostile intent. Can you offer me protection if necessary?"

"We'll be glad to, little fellow," Westfield said. "I'll protect you any way necessary."

"Oh man," I mumbled. "I think I understand what happened. I think that magnetic field must have scrambled his code. He's, like, at some primitive default mode, or something. He sounds like a little robot."

"That's all he is anyway," Julie commented. "A pseudo-sophisticated little robot."

"Should we check out the others?" I asked. "I might be able to get through to one of the others."

Westfield nodded to Julie, and she pulled the other cards out of the magnetic freezer where they had been stored. Jack sat down on the table, his knees bent before him. "The alien life form is staring at me," he announced. "Staring is a sign of hostile intentions in carbon-based life forms except possibly during mating season, when it may have other meanings."

The two guards had been watching Jack with interest. But now they sat back on the sofa and yawned.

"Not bad. B minus. C plus," one of them said.

"It's not as good as the singing trout you have on your wall," the other replied.

During the lull in activity, Sam nudged me and pointed to a nicely framed document that hung on the wall. It looked like the name of a business or a corporation.

Haul-Over Biotec Options.

Sam was mouthing something silently.

"All right, let's give it a try," David Westfield said, gesturing to the pile of cards on the table.

"I have the last one right here," Julie said, then suddenly she screamed.

52

Lex and Nim had burst into the room, and Lex was swinging his guitar like a club. He smashed one guard on the head, then the other, while Nim slammed into Julie, mushing her against the magnetic freezer. Sam had jumped on David and was biting his wrist.

"Take that, you sick little hobo!" he screamed.

David dropped the stun gun, and I picked it up, fiddled with it a moment, and managed somehow to shoot him in the knee. David shrieked and fell to the floor.

"The cards!" Nim called. I scooped them up, Jack hopped up onto my shoulder, and the four of us spun out the door and took off like deer down the sandy road.

"Those two guys are coming after us!" Nim called out between clenched teeth.

Lex was a fast runner, and he got to the Wagoneer before the rest of us. He backed it out and we all piled in. Lex fumbled with the shift, and we shot ahead across the soft sand. He glanced in the rear-view mirror.

"Duck!" he called.

"Duck!" Nim repeated.

Sam screamed something senseless that sounded like "Goose!"

I pushed Sam down as a bullet whistled overhead. It smashed through the windshield, leaving a hole the size of a nickel. But that was it. The Wagoneer went over a hill and around a curve, and we were out of range.

"Hurry!" Nim called. "They're gonna get their truck."

"No way they'll catch this baby!" Lex replied, downshifting as we hit the hard sand by the water. We were going so fast the waves seemed to blur together.

For a few minutes no one said anything. Lex flicked on the headlights.

Jack was peering out cautiously from the collar of my shirt.

"Are you okay?" I asked him.

"A bit shaken up, but otherwise fine," Jack replied.

"Hey, you got your normal voice back!" Sam exclaimed.

"Yes, that was all an act, you see," Jack remarked.

"We had a pre-arranged signal," I explained. "If I ask him, 'How are you feeling?' he denies he knows me."

"But the robot talk was my own personal inspiration," Jack added.

"That was awesome!" I told him. "You almost had me convinced."

"You said mean things about me. You said I was stupid. Why'd you say all those mean things about me?" Sam asked, in his fake whiny voice. He had his charming little-boy smile on his face.

"Sometimes you're a little *too* convincing, the way you play the dumb younger brother," I replied.

"I *was* stupid for a minute there," Sam admitted. "But I'm also the one who figured out what HOBO meant."

"Yeah, what was that all about? Why'd you scream 'hobo' at David Westfield?" Nim asked.

"The name of his company. Haul-Over Biotec Options. HOBO."

"OMG," Nim said. "So Westfield was sending the messages all along?" she asked.

"Yeah," Sam replied. "That's why he kept telling us to look for someone with expertise and spill out our secrets to him. He was playing on our trust."

"Nice work," I said.

"You did okay yourself, bro. Nifty plan in there." Sam explained to the others how I had made David Westfield think we were really there to help him.

"As long as the compliments are flowing, I have to say, good guitar work, Lex," I told him.

"My first smash hit," he responded.

Nim brought the palm of her hand to her forehead. "You left your guitar back there!" she exclaimed.

"No matter, it's broken up now anyway," Lex said. "A little help for my friends."

She gave him a look that was so full of affection and admiration, I thought I might be sick.

53

When we came to our street, Nim glanced about nervously.

"What now?" she asked. "There's nowhere we're safe anymore. And nowhere for your mom, either." She pointed toward the house. "Wait—what's going on there?"

Three police cars were parked in front of our house, and a bunch of policemen were milling around. As we pulled up, one of them approached the car and held up his hand. I placed Jack in my pocket with the other cards.

"Oh boy!" Nim said. "Here comes the part about having no driver's license."

The officer's beefy face appeared at the window. But instead of questioning us, he simply nodded hello and motioned to Lex to pull into the driveway.

As we parked he came over and pointed at the hole in the windshield.

"Looks like you saw a little action," he said. "Is everyone okay?"

Nim explained about the two men and the pickup truck. The policeman ordered us all inside immediately. He put in a call to headquarters. A few policemen remained outside, apparently to protect us.

Mom was seated on a chair facing the door. "Thank God!" she exclaimed, jumping to her feet and opening her arms. Her eyes were red, and she looked exhausted. Brinda pushed up to us, wagging her tail. She sniffed at our hands and arms with quick puffs and seemed offended at having been left behind.

"We got the cards," I said proudly.

"You see, it *was* all right to let the children go," Curtis told Mom. As usual, he seemed slightly detached from his surroundings, like a blimp floating above the landscape—and oddly, it struck me for the first time as a likable trait.

"You will not put yourself at risk again," Mom declared. She discovered the marks on Sam's face where he had been struck, and she let out a little cry. His face was a mess. She hugged him and took him into the bathroom to care for his wounds.

I carried the cards into the living room and set them down on the rug. Brinda trotted after me and waited nearby.

The card people came to their feet solemnly and met in a circle. Brinda watched them for a minute, her tail wagging. When she saw they were busy, she lay down, lifted her ears once or twice, and was still. By now, most of the cards were out, and most of them were weeping. In addition to the Ten of Clubs and the Queen of Spades, they had lost seven other cards—the Ace of Hearts and six children. Forty-two of the original fifty-two cards still remained.

The King and Queen of Hearts spoke to the grieving cards, praising the good and noble traits of those they had lost. The Ten of Clubs' great gusto and bravery in piloting the first electric car and the Queen of Spades' wise philosophic musings were among the virtues that they mentioned. They stood and bowed their heads in silence.

54

During a break in the ceremony, Sam, Mom, and Curtis came silently into the room and sat down against the wall. Brinda pulled herself to her feet and slouched over to them, and Curtis put his arm around her.

Sam's lips were swollen like he'd had a Botox treatment, and there were some pretty ugly cuts and scrapes on his cheeks. There was bruising around his eyes, too. They had worked him over pretty good.

The cards stood, came together once more in a daisy shape, touched their heads, and finally pulled apart. Not long afterwards, the two remaining Aces fluttered out the windows. Others stood about, hugging one another and talking. Some of the Clubs children gathered on a side table, pointing at a picture on the wall of early aviators and their airplanes.

"Amazing," Curtis remarked. "They seem to feel emotions and curiosity, just like humans."

"And why shouldn't they?" Lex asked.

"Do I know you?" Curtis asked, rather abruptly. Lex apologized for not introducing himself. They rose to their feet and shook hands—both of them standing so stiffly and formally that it was comical. Lex meant it to be funny and Curtis was, well, just being Curtis.

"What surprises me is their resemblance to carbon-based life forms," Curtis went on. "I knew that Samir was working hard to create them with all the many attributes of humans and other animals . . . but to have genuine emotion is something I didn't expect."

"You didn't do a bad job with their logic, either," Mom told him.

"Oh, to be sure," he replied. "But logic is itself quite logical. How did Samir give them emotions? How did he give these creatures . . . hearts?"

"They have more than hearts," Sam declared. His lips were so swollen, it seemed to hurt him to talk.

"They do?" Curtis asked, with a puzzled look.

"Oh yeah. The Jack of Diamonds has the hots for Nim," Sam told him. "That guy has some serious stones."

"Shut up, Sam!" Nim told him.

"Should I be jealous?" Lex teased, and Nim turned away and crossed her arms.

Curtis and Mom listened intently as we filled them in on the details of the past few days. At one point Curtis patted his hip. "Samir warned me I might need this," he mumbled. He stood by the front window and looked out at the street, where the police stood silent guard.

Mom shuddered at my description of the scissors attack in math class.

"Why haven't they come here again?" she asked.

Proud of his new knowledge, Sam explained the magnetic field that the card people had used to disable the most recent generation of scissors people.

"Westfield will find a way to undo that," Mom said. "And then what? If one of them can try to attack you in school, what will a whole group of them be able to do?"

Jack had hopped up onto my shoulder and stood there listening, tilting his head from side to side like a cat.

"May I offer some thoughts?" he asked.

"Of course," Mom said. She stuck out her finger and poked him gently. "By the way, thank you for being Paul's and Sam's special friend."

"Thanks to you and your husband for creating such a fine batch of DNA," Jack replied, smiling. "But to the matter at hand. The scissors people are more primitive than we are. Ironically, their lack of civilizing restraint is an important source of their strength. Murdering a hundred thousand people is no different to them than wounding one."

He paused a moment. "They can also self-replicate—an ability that we have been denied. And with David Westfield working closely with them, there is little doubt that they will find a way to replicate themselves in horrible quantities—not too far in the future."

Sam and I groaned. Curtis looked on grimly.

"What can we do?" Mom asked Jack.

"Right now the Spades are putting the final touches on a new plan."

"We're eager to hear it," Curtis told him.

"Soon," Jack replied.

Off to one side of the room, the card children were cutting out cardboard, bending it, and shaping it onto a frame.

"I think those little guys are constructing a flying machine," Lex said.

"OMG, it is!" Nim exclaimed. "Look how nicely rounded those wings are!"

"Can't you just say 'Oh my God'?" Lex asked her. "It's a little more mature."

She stuck her tongue out at him, and he laughed and tried to take her hand, but she pulled away. She slipped out into the hall, her lips pulled forward in a pout.

A few minutes later I was passing through the hall on my way to the kitchen, and she stopped me and began right away to complain about Lex. "He treats me like a kid sometimes. I hate it when he does that. It's not like I'm two years old."

"I think he's pretty nice to you, all things considered," I told her.

She frowned. "What's that supposed to mean?" She looked past me. "Oh, hi," she said, in a voice that sounded hurt and friendly at the same time.

Lex had come out to look for her. "Listen, Nim . . . you don't need to get upset over every little thing."

She crossed her arms and turned away. Lex gave me a look, and I wandered out to the kitchen and had a snack.

When I went upstairs to my computer, I found another message waiting for me from the HOBO (which of course, meant David Westfield).

Final Thought 2

You might think it's over, but we've only begun.

The battle continues till one side has won.

All the good feeling from the rescue shriveled up like roses in a winter frost.

55

About an hour later, the card people were ready to try out their airplane. For the runway they had chosen the long hallway from the back door. The Jack of Clubs was given the honor of being the first pilot. He sat up high in the front of the vehicle, wearing tiny old-fashioned aviator's goggles, made out of reused plastic packaging, and a soft crash helmet molded from dryer lint. As with the electric car, the Clubs children were the power source. They stood in a circle in the cabin, their hands joined around a magnetic bar. A small plastic propeller, borrowed from one of Sam's old rubber-band powered gliders, was attached to the front of the airplane. The wings, sturdy and nicely tapered, stretched about a foot to either side of the fuselage.

"Power on!" the Jack of Clubs called, and the blade started to turn. The airplane lurched forward on its rubber wheels, borrowed from one of Sam's old battery cars.

The Jack of Clubs pushed down a lever, the airplane rolled faster and faster down the runway, it skipped once on its wheels—and then with a gentle hum it was airborne, lifting up above our heads as it entered the living room. The card people's cheers echoed down the hallway like the spring song of peepers. The airplane was just banking and turning back towards the hall when something silver and black shot in through the window and skewered the airplane down the middle, sending broken bits of cards flying off in all directions. The remains of the flying machine fell with a sickening crunch to the wood floor, splintering into little pieces of cardboard and plastic. The scissors bounced off a wall and sailed once around the room, as if taking a victory lap or surveying the damage they had caused, and then shot back out through the window.

Moments later the Ace of Spades fluttered into the room, darted about chaotically, and landed on the back of a cane chair, trembling like a wounded butterfly. It took flight once more, but faltered, and, with a twirling motion like a maple seed, it fell to the floor and landed on its back, never again to stir.

56

Mom collapsed onto the sofa and buried her face in her hands. Sam and I squatted on the floor, picking up the pieces of what was left of the airplane and the Clubs children. Over by the door, Nim and Lex were holding hands and talking to a policeman who had seen the shattered window and wondered if a rifle or cannon of some sort had been fired into the house. Curtis joined them and explained it must have been a shot from a rifle, which sent the police off to scour the neighborhood.

We all knew we had to keep the card people secret.

Jack emerged from an emergency meeting with the Spades and requested an immediate conference with us.

We sat in a semi-circle on the living room floor, surrounded by bits of glass and plastic.

"The Kings and Queens have approved a plan," Jack informed us, "and now it is up to you." He glanced toward me.

"What's your idea, Jack?" I asked.

"These are desperate times," Jack began. "Minutes ago, we lost three more Club children as well as the Jack of Clubs and the Ace of Spades, which reduces our total to thirty-seven. Our numbers are diminishing at a time when our foe's power is growing at an alarming rate. At least one of the scissors people is out of magnetic lock, and more will follow. With David

Westfield's help, their destructive power will soon be immense—literally world-shattering."

"What do they want?" Sam asked. "Why are they doing this?"

Curtis leaned forward. "Like all intensely selfish people, Westfield probably started off wanting money and power," he explained. "But by now, he's been caught in a web of his own making. The terrorist group that funds him is certainly calling the shots now. Which raises all sorts of awful scenarios."

"How can we stop it?" Mom asked.

"Blow 'em up!" Lex exclaimed. "Bring in the military! Blast that whole section of the Haul-over to oblivion!"

"Now, young man . . ." Curtis began.

"Blow up that David guy, and Julie too, while you're at it!" Lex continued.

There was a pause.

"It wouldn't work, Lex," Curtis told him, in a quiet voice.

"Why not?" Lex glanced over at me, as if for support.

I tried to explain. "What if they have their supplies of nanodust hidden on the Haul-over?" I pointed out. "You know . . . the bad nanodust?"

"Exactly," Curtis replied. "An explosion would spread it across the entire state. And then . . ."

"Living nightmare," Sam proclaimed. "Holy horrors. Knives that fly through the air. Corkscrews that drill down into your brain."

"OMG," Nim murmured.

"Yeah, yeah, okay," Lex said, waving his hand. "I get it. Bad idea. Go on."

Jack swiveled his head a bit. "I heard once that desperate times call for desperate remedies. Our new plan *is* quite desperate—but that might work to our advantage.

"We believe our best chance to avert tragedy is to strike where they least expect it. Where they are brutal and strong, we need to be weak and defenseless." Jack drew himself to his full height. "We propose to infiltrate the scissors people and infect them."

"You mean to infect them with a virus—something that will kill them off?" Mom asked.

"A virus—yes. But not to kill. They would know how to repel a direct attack."

"So you're just going to give them a common cold or something?" Sam asked.

Jack raised a finger in the air. "We believe it might be possible to *alter* the scissors people in significant ways without alerting their defenses. We think we can infect their code and modify it in small, subtle ways."

"Take away their cruelty," I said.

"Precisely."

"Brilliant," Curtis declared. He paused. "Yes, it's the best way."

No one said anything for a few moments. Then Mom asked, "How will you give them the 'good' virus without their knowing it?"

"That's exactly what I need to talk to you all about," Jack replied. "In order to infiltrate them undetected, I myself will need to be altered quite substantially."

Curtis nodded in agreement. "For one thing, you'll need to have your own external restraints taken away. Those are too easy for the scissors people to detect." He stood up and paced around the room, his hand to his chin. For some reason now, his awkwardness struck me as almost lovable.

"What's external restraints?" Sam asked.

"It's an layer of coding that was built as a buffer around the card people to prevent them from harming carbon-based life forms," Curtis told him. Sam gave me a look that said, *Do you understand what they're talking about?*

Jack nodded. "It seems that the scissors people can virtually *smell* the restraints in our code. They brand us as something different, something alien—an enemy."

Curtis frowned. "Assuming that we can remove your restraints, it raises another vexing question," he said.

"What question?" Mom asked.

"I think I know," I interjected.

Curtis smiled slightly. "Okay, Paul. Proceed."

I chose my words carefully. "The question is, if he has no built-in restraints, will Jack become just another scissors person—just as cruel and bloodthirsty—only smarter and more powerful?"

"Yes, that's it," Curtis replied.

"I've thought about this myself," Jack announced.

"And?" I asked.

Jack shrugged. "No one knows. We can only hope that without the restraints, my basic nature is still good." Brinda came over and sniffed at him where he perched on my shoulder. He reached down and petted her large brown nose. "The question is, darling, have I been nice to you because I had to, or because I really love you with a heart that is true?"

57

How much time did we have before the next attack by the scissors people?

We soon received an answer. The last remaining Ace, the Ace of Clubs, returned that afternoon with the results of its most recent surveillance. The King of Hearts relayed the news, and it was better than we had feared. There would be no more attacks for at least a few days and possibly longer. David Westfield had taken all the available force from the scissors people and channeled it into the pair of scissors that attacked the airplane. It had expended every last bit of its energy in its attack and was barely able to complete its flight back home across the bay. In the meantime, David Westfield had rigged up a charging device for all the scissors, but it would take a few days for them to reach full strength. He was also devising some sort of chamber for full-scale replication of the scissors people.

We had some time, but we had to move quickly. Nim called her mother and asked for permission to stay at our house for the next few days; Mom told Sam and me that we could skip school; Lex talked to his grandfather and said he needed to remain here to help with a family issue. We were all in.

At Mom's insistence, the police visited David Westfield at his vacation cottage on the Haul-over. Two officers drove there in the police SUV the next afternoon and found Westfield highly cooperative. He insisted on giving them a tour of his laboratory and told them all about his research into new, super-light, super-strong metal that promised to revolutionize future US military aircraft. By way of example, he showed them a simple pair of scissors—light, durable, great cutting edges. Very impressed, and not a little charmed by his warmth, intelligence, and openness, the officers drove back to headquarters and filed a favorable report.

For countless hours over the past few days, Curtis had been working at his computer on a little table in Dad's study, poring over the codes of the card people. The rest of us were in the living room. I was playing thirty-seven card solitaire, and at difficult points in the game, with a quick exchange of winks, the card people silently rearranged their positions so I could win.

"It's the least we can do," the Jack of Diamonds joked, "considering that you're not playing with a full deck." He glanced longingly toward Nim.

Late that evening, Curtis came into the living room. "I believe I have located the section of code that we need to remove."

"I still don't really get it," Sam complained. "What exactly do you have to remove?" The cuts and bruises on his cheeks and around his eyes look pretty impressive now. They'd swelled up and turned dark purple over the past few days, and his lips were as puffy as little sausages.

"As we discussed, the restraint section must go," Curtis explained to him, "the section that forbids the card people to harm carbon-based creatures."

"Well, would they *want* to hurt creatures like us?" Sam asked.

"That's what we don't know."

"Do we have a section like that in *our* code?"

"Sam, people don't have a code," Nim told him. "We have DNA, which gives us instincts, and then—well—I don't know."

"What stops us from hurting other creatures?" Sam went on.

Everyone was silent.

"That's a good question, dude," Lex told him. "Like, I don't really know the answer to that. The law, maybe?"

"Hmm, I don't know," Mom said. "It's probably a combination of our ability to feel empathy for others and . . . and our upbringing, I suppose. Not all people grow up with kindness, and it shows."

"But is kindness stored in us as a code?" Sam asked.

"What you're asking," Curtis paraphrased, "is, when people have a *heart*, is it a series of commands that they must follow, or is it something more flexible and innate—a kind of goodness that is central to their being and radiates out into everything they do?"

Nim looked at Curtis with a beautiful light in her eyes. "You said that really well," she told him.

Curtis bowed slightly.

Sam pursed his lips. "Yeah, I guess that's what I'm asking," he told Curtis.

"Not everyone has a heart. You have to grow it," I declared.

For a moment there was silence.

"I'm curious, honey—how do we *grow* a heart?" Mom asked.

I looked down at my hands—that bad habit of mine. "When you love someone and you lose them, and you still love them anyway . . . that's what gives you a heart." I felt everyone sort of leaning in toward me. Mom's eyes were glistening. I looked up and added, "We'd better hope Jack has a heart, because if he doesn't . . ."

Jack was watching with interest. "Well, here's an example," he said. He bent over and picked up a cricket that was hiding under the radiator. "Come on, little fellow." Cradling it under his arm, he carried it to the back door. "You see, I had to do it," he told Sam when he came back. "I had no choice. But what will I do when I have the choice?"

"I get it now. Dad gave you training wheels, and Curtis is going to take them off to see if you can ride with the big boys," Sam said, with a little smile.

58

The surgery was scheduled for later that evening. First, Curtis had to bring back some equipment from the lab—which he did with a police escort. At eight-thirty he carried a large cardboard box into the kitchen. On Mom's slate island in the middle of the room, he set it all up: a bunch of dials and wires and copper leads, and a round instrument that looked like some sort of tuning device. Jack watched calmly.

"It's best if I do the surgery while you are fully conscious," Curtis told Jack, "the way doctors perform some types of brain surgery on humans. That way I can tell if I've hit the right subprogram."

"Your call, Doc," Jack replied.

"I think all us spectators should leave the room," Nim said. "Surgery is such a private thing."

"I'd like to have Paul here," Jack said. "For moral support."

"Sure," I said. "No blood, though," I joked. "I don't do well at the sight of blood."

"No blood," Jack agreed with a smile.

Curtis fastened Jack down on a strip of copper metal with some black elastic bands. He attached an electrode to each shoulder and plugged those wires into his laptop. After he hit a few buttons, a window opened on the screen and a long series of code scrolled up through the window.

"We have a very detailed picture of your inner workings here, Mr. Jack," Curtis told him.

"How's my heart?" Jack asked.

"Made of gold." Curtis gave a tiny smile.

This was a first: Curtis was actually going along with a joke. But then he got serious again.

"All right, I would like to try a few tests on you."

He highlighted a section of code and pressed an activation command. "Wait a minute," he said. "Nothing's happening." He pushed some more buttons. He shook his head and stared at the screen. "Darn!" He hit one button several times in a row. More headshaking.

"Your code is locked, Jack," he said. "I can't get into it."

"No surprise there," Jack replied, "given the care with which the program was written. Could there be a DNA match? We have Paul right here."

"No, this one isn't a DNA match," Curtis replied. "There must be a password or other activator." Curtis fumbled around a bit more. "Wait a minute—I found the sub-program. Yes, it's a password, and there's a prompt here to remind us what it is."

I came up beside him and looked over his shoulder. "What's the prompt?"

Curtis hit some more keys. "Here it is: *How would I like to come back to life?*"

Bingo. "That's easy," I replied, remembering what Dad had told me.

"You think you know it?" Curtis asked.

"Yes, I know it. *As a plum.*"

"As a plum?" Curtis asked, a little skeptically.

"Yes."

"Three separate words?"

"I think so."

"Interesting answer. Let's see if it works."

Curtis typed in the password. The screen scrolled up and down and stabilized again. "Success!" he declared. "We're in! Okay, Jack, here comes test number one."

He highlighted the section of code again, pressed the buttons to activate it, and looked over at Jack.

"Run!" Jack screamed. "Run for your life!"

Curtis deactivated the section. "Okay, flight response is where we thought it would be."

"That was intense," Jack said. "I was running on a treadmill, and a scissors person was flying after me."

"Let's see what happens this time." Curtis scrolled up the screen to another section of code and activated it.

Jack turned his head and looked at me. "Have I told you recently how much I love you?" he asked.

"Uh, not really," I replied, smiling.

"Having you there for me . . . You're like a brother to me, man."

Curtis deactivated the code. "Affection centers are where we thought."

"I meant it all," Jack explained. "It's just, you know, a little embarrassing to say those things out loud."

"It's all good," I replied.

"One more little test," Curtis said. He scrolled around for a minute or two, found another section of code, and activated it.

"Actually, no," Jack asserted. "Not in the slightest. There is absolutely no evidence that the use of coffee is harmful to the human body."

"Deactivated," Curtis announced. "That was one of the centers of cognition and argumentation."

"Who knows where that came from?" Jack asked. "I don't even drink coffee."

"All right," Curtis said. "All the tests have been successful. We're good to go."

Jack blinked and tipped his head, first to one side, then to the other. "I'm ready."

"I don't think this will hurt," Curtis told him, "but you may experience a little ping or possibly a brief sensation of darkness." Slowly, carefully, he zeroed in on a long section of code, placing markers at the front and back. He wrote a few new lines and pasted them in at the beginning. Then he highlighted the code between the markers.

"Are you ready?" he asked Jack.

"I'm ready," Jack declared.

Curtis hit the delete button and the section of code shivered off into hyperspace.

Jack's head turned slowly from side to side. "Didn't feel a thing," he declared.

"Excellent," Curtis replied.

Jack gazed up at Curtis. "You have a really funny nose," he said. "It starts off in one direction and ends up in the other."

"I have what's referred to as a 'deviated septum,'" Curtis replied.

"Sep*tum*? I'm thinking more along the lines of sep*tic*. I mean, your breath smells like raw sewage. Man! Have you ever heard of breath mints?"

Curtis raised his eyebrows and glanced over at me.

59

"Do you detect some new behavior?" Curtis asked.

I nodded.

Jack turned to me. "What's the matter with you? Did your mouth fall open, or are you trying to catch a fly?"

"I'm a little surprised by the changes in you, Jack," I said.

"What's the matter? Can't a guy say what he thinks?"

"Actually, not *all* the time."

Jack waved an arm dismissively and shook his head.

Curtis spoke again. "Jack, I'm going to ask you to remain very quiet and still, while I deactivate the program and disconnect you."

"You'd be screaming like a plucked chicken if I ran my fingers through *your* innards," Jack retorted. But he lay there as Curtis closed down the program and then carefully detached the electrodes.

"Okay, you're free," Curtis said.

Jack stood up and stretched his arms and legs. "That was weird," he commented. He strolled around the slate countertop, shaking out his arms like a wrestler before a match. "All righty then," he commented, looking about. He had a restless gleam in his eye.

A brown moth was fluttering through the air in his direction. Jack crouched down, and as it came overhead, he leaped into the air and grabbed it. The moth struggled mightily against him, flapping its wings and pushing at him with its little black feet, but Jack brought it down to the slate and fell on top of it with a crunch. The moth writhed back and forth and then was still, and when Jack stood up, it remained as still as a piece of crumpled paper.

"You just killed a living creature," Curtis told him.

"So what?" Jack replied. "I hate those things. They smell like wet wool, and they're always bumping into me and my people."

"Did you expect this much of a change?" I asked Curtis.

Curtis shook his head. "I had no expectations."

As Curtis began to put the equipment away, Jack hopped up onto my shoulder. "What's your problem?" he asked.

"No problem," I replied.

"Don't lie to me. It's as clear as the decaying mass of organic material inside you that you've got a problem with me."

"Jack, what about being kind to others?" I reminded him. "What about showing concern for other life forms?"

"Do other life forms show any concern for me?" Jack asked. "Humans, for instance. They strap us down and torture us and then put a blowtorch to us . . . gee, why can't I be as nice to humans as they are to me and my people?"

"There might be some truth in what you said," I replied. "But does that give you or me the right to be unkind?"

"I'm tuning you out, Reverend."

"What can I do to help you?" I asked.

"Well, you could carry me into the other room. Or are you going to make me walk?"

"I'll carry you."

With Jack perched on my shoulder like a surfer, I stepped into the other room and sat down on the sofa. "Mission accomplished," I said quietly. Everyone smiled and applauded.

Jack hopped off my shoulder. "What's the matter with all of you?" he asked, with a definite bite in his voice. "You think this is some sort of freak show? Or are you just happy that I'm willing to risk my own life to save yours from the snappin' scissors?"

His statement was greeted by stunned silence. Around the room, the other card people stopped what they were doing and turned toward Jack to watch.

"Jack," Nim asked, "are you angry about something?"

"Oh no, sister, not at all. I mean, why should I be angry?" he replied sarcastically. "Just because we card people sacrifice our lives again and again to save you? Does any human ever show any willingness to make a sacrifice?"

"My husband gave you your life," Mom told him. "He gave his lifetime of work for you. What more could you ask?" She stared at him.

Jack waved his arm dismissively. "Oh, I know, the noble, the wonderful, the brilliant scientist Samir Kapadia. As if humans have any place in the future world."

"Why wouldn't humans have a place in the future?" Nim asked.

"Yeah, we created you!" Sam added.

"Well la de da!" Jack replied sarcastically. "The grotesquely deformed little brother speaks!" He hopped down onto the table in front of the sofa and did a little gymnastics routine— some flips and a twirl through the air.

Watching from a side table, the Jack of Spades put his head in his hands and shook his head. "It's terribly depressing to look into our hearts like this," he lamented. "Not at all what I expected."

Curtis appeared in the doorway. He looked anxious and agitated. "I made a mistake," he announced.

60

We all looked up at Curtis.

"A serious mistake. I added a few codes to re-direct his consciousness around the vanished code . . . but by mistake, the new code sends him right to the aggression center."

"I'll say," Mom told him.

"I need to perform one more procedure to fix the new code."

Jack had turned his head toward Curtis and was listening. "Think again, buddy! You're not getting me under the knife again!" And with that, he hopped onto the floor and raced off across the room toward the kitchen.

"Come back here, Jack!" I yelled. Sam, Nim, and I jumped to our feet.

"Fear not, humans! We'll get him!" the Jack of Diamonds declared, and with a mighty leap from a side table, he landed on the floor, followed by several other cards. They streamed down the hall like a river and disappeared into the kitchen.

A minute later Sam was lying on his side on the kitchen floor.

"He's under here!" he yelled. "He went under the fridge!"

With the Jack of Diamonds at the head of one group, and the Jack of Spades at the head of the other, the cards split up and swarmed in from opposite sides.

A few minutes later they reappeared, carrying Jack. He was kicking and screaming and flailing at them with his arms. "Put me down, you traitors!" he yelled. "Put me down or I'll blast you into hyperspace!"

The Queen of Hearts walked grandly into the room and stood in front of them, throwing her cloak behind her. "Release him!" she commanded.

The Jack of Diamonds and Jack of Spades looked up at her and motioned to the other cards to let Jack go.

Jack stood there, swiveling his head on his flexible neck and darting quick glances around the room.

"Come here!" the Queen commanded.

Jack walked forward sulkily. He was littered still with the gray fluffy stuff that gathers under refrigerators.

"Look at me when you approach me!" she commanded.

Jack lifted his head, still scowling, but he looked at her.

"Now kneel in front of me!" she ordered.

Jack knelt before her on the tile floor. One of the Hearts children ran up and gave him a quick dusting off.

"I don't care what surgery was done on you, or how it may have addled your cognitive powers—but you will not disgrace the card people! Is that clear?"

"Yes, your highness," Jack responded. He bowed lower.

"Now you will walk back under your own power to the surgery table, lay yourself down, and prepare yourself for the procedure. And I will not hear one word of complaint from you."

"Yes, your majesty," Jack replied.

"Now rise to your feet and do as I ordered! And remember the proud people whom you represent!" With a magnificent toss of her head, the Queen of Hearts turned and exited the room. The Two, Three, Five and Six of Hearts raced up to carry her train for her so it didn't drag along the floor.

61

Jack waited for her to go and then, in silence, he climbed up onto the slate countertop and lay down on the surgery table. Curtis fastened him down again with the black elastic bands and connected the electrodes.

"All right, Jack, this won't take long," he said. Jack made a little face at him.

"Patience, Jack," I counseled.

If eyes the size of sesame seeds can roll, his eyes rolled.

Curtis hit a few keystrokes. He watched as the code streamed up onto the screen and stabilized, and he typed in the password. Some more quick keystrokes and he was done.

"There," he told me. "That directs him back to the executive function instead of activating the aggression center. I can't promise everything will be perfect, but let's see . . ."

He removed the electrodes and took off the elastic bands.

"Well," said Jack, sitting up. "That wasn't so bad." He hopped up onto his feet.

"You look like you feel better now," I said.

"I do."

"Talk about having a chip on your shoulder!"

"Being angry all the time isn't what it's cracked up to be," Jack remarked. "It gets tiresome."

"We noticed," Curtis told him.

Jack scurried up onto my shoulder. While Curtis put away the equipment again, I brought Jack back into the living room.

This time no one applauded when we walked in.

Jack hopped down onto the table in front of the sofa and began to stride back and forth. Then he stopped and spoke. "I wish to apologize for my earlier behavior. It was unbecoming of a card person and offensive to our human friends. I especially apologize to you, Mrs. Kapadia, for the degrading remarks I made about your husband."

"I accept your apology," Mom replied.

Two of the youngest Diamonds hopped up onto the table and pointed at Jack.

"You were funny when you ran away!" the Three of Diamonds said in his little-boy voice.

"Do it again!" lisped the Two of Diamonds.

"Yuck, what's happening to me?!" Jack exclaimed.

Brinda had come up beside him and was sniffing at him with her shiny, dimpled nose.

"Oh gross, you're all wet! Get away from me!" Jack told her, pushing her nose so hard that Brinda whimpered and fell back onto her hind legs.

"Jack!" scolded the Queen of Hearts from across the room. "Remember who you are!"

"Yes, your majesty," Jack replied. He shook his head. "I don't know what came over me," he said. "I'm sorry, Brinda. Come here, girl, I'm very sorry!"

Brinda gave him a quick glance, turned, and head hanging, walked away. Though he called to her to come, she pretended not to hear.

"The aggression centers might still present a challenge," Curtis commented, as Nim and Lex nodded.

Jack sat down. He gazed about with a perplexed air. "Yes, but what can I do about it?" he asked.

"You need to learn how to behave," Sam told him. "Just like us kids, you need to learn how to control yourself."

"What if the scissors people make you angry?" Nim asked. "How will you be able to survive if you get blinded with rage?"

Jack listened with interest. "How do humans learn to control their behavior?" he asked.

"Practice, like in a sport," Sam said.

"Go with our noblest feelings," Nim asserted.

"Be logical at all times," Curtis explained.

"Play music," Lex remarked.

"Keep faith in the goodness of life, no matter what," Mom advised.

"Remember the people we love," I recalled.

Jack tilted his head. "It's a very complicated thing to be a human, isn't it?" he asked.

62

Early the next morning, after a quick breakfast, we split up into two teams and began Jack's training in self-control. Sam and Lex had to find ways to frustrate and anger Jack. Nim and I had to come up with some strategies to help him overcome those feelings.

Nim and I met first with Jack in my room to preview a few strategies.

"Okay, Jack," Nim said. "Let's say you're mad at someone, what are you going to do?"

"Hmmm, I don't know," Jack said. He glanced up at her. "Give me an example."

"Let's say Brinda comes up to you and sniffs at you with her wet nose and gets you all slimy," I suggested.

Jack's face turned bright red, and his motions grew quick and agitated.

"I'd smack her!" he exclaimed. "There's nothing I hate more than getting dog slime all over my beautiful royal clothing!" He strode about with exaggerated motions of his legs and arms.

"Wrong answer!" Nim told him.

Jack stopped and turned to her. "Oh. Yes, I can see that."

"Here's what you do instead: You remind yourself that Brinda is a friend of yours, and that she loves you, and that she would do anything to help you, including possibly putting her own life in danger. Instead of pushing her away, you ask her politely to move back and give you some space."

"Let me try that," Jack said. He closed his little eyes and pressed his hand to his forehead. He opened his eyes again. "Okay, got it," he said. "Shall we give it a try?"

Brinda was lying down in Sam's room. I called to her, and she trotted in, wagging her tail, and nuzzled my hands. Her ears perked up when she saw Jack, who stood facing away from her. She seemed to have forgiven him for the rough treatment of the previous night. She sniffed at him once and then started swiping him with her wet tongue.

Jack shivered, raised an arm, and cupped his hand into a fist . . . and then slowly, he loosened his fist and let his arm fall to his side. He took a step back.

"I love you, darling," he cooed, petting her nose. "But will you please hold off a bit and give me a little space? I'm not quite myself this morning."

Brinda gave a snort, wagged her tail, and backed slowly off. She sat, looked up at Jack once more with a quizzical expression, and finally lay down, resting her head elegantly on her paws.

"Well done, Jack!" I exclaimed. "You just mastered your first lesson!"

Jack cleared his throat. "There's a small issue with my clothes," he pointed out. Nim found a tissue and wiped Jack down as he stood at attention.

"Thank you," he told her.

Sam and Lex were standing nearby, watching. "Are you ready for lesson *numero dos*, Jack my man?" Lex asked.

"Oh, I suppose so, Lex my man," Jack replied. "What will happen this time—will I be tossed into a toilet?"

"Are you saying that's where you belong?" Sam came back.

Jack turned toward Sam and placed his hands on his hips. "And what exactly do you mean by that, may I ask?" he demanded.

Yes, both Jack and Sam had some work to do.

The lessons for the rest of the morning involved put-downs, patience, frustration, and living with physical discomfort. We took a lunch break, and Jack went off to be with the other cards, where he practiced his new skills. After lunch, we tried out some more advanced and challenging versions of the morning's lessons. Though Jack still slipped here and there, he was making good progress.

Mom came out of her bedroom from time to time to watch.

"How did you children become such good teachers?" she asked.

"They must have had good parents," Nim responded.

"You're the real natural. You're a born teacher," I told Nim.

Mom's smile lingered on me a moment. She went back to her room to lie down again.

63

With police protection, Curtis had been at his office all day, working on the virus—the code splice—that Jack would use to infect the scissors people. When he came to the house at the end of the day, we showed him some of the day's lessons with Jack, and he pursed his lips and nodded in approval. "How difficult is it for you to remember these strategies?" he asked Jack.

"It's hard work," Jack said. "The aggressive center is surprisingly strong. Why did Samir Kapadia bother to include that in my personality, do you think?"

"My guess is, he knew you wouldn't be able to defend yourself without it," Curtis conjectured. "All creatures need to have an anger response of some sort in order to mobilize against threats."

After working all day with me, Nim had gone over to sit with Lex. With a shiver of pain, I watched her place her hand on top of his. I tried to remind myself that I liked Lex. The shiver didn't go away.

Suddenly Sam stood up and threw his hands into the air.

"Hold everything!" he exclaimed.

Everyone stopped what they were doing and looked at him.

"What's wrong, Sammy?" Nim asked.

"Don't 'Sammy' me!" he told her.

"Remember your strategies," Jack counseled.

"All right, all right. Listen, everybody, there's something really, really wrong with this plan," Sam said. "Am I the only one who sees it?"

I smiled. This seemed to be Sam's specialty, finding what was "wrong" with our plans.

"What's wrong?" Curtis asked.

"Well, you took away the 'external restraint' program because you say the scissors people would have recognized it right away—you said they would have smelled it or something, right?" Sam asked.

"Correct," Curtis replied.

"Yeah, and so now you think they won't be able to tell that Jack is different from them?"

"Yes. Despite Jack's greater sophistication, we hope that he will present to them as the same basic, hostile being that they are."

"Yeah, well there's something really obvious that we're missing here, people!"

Everyone looked toward him.

"What are we missing, Sammy . . . uh, Sam?" Nim asked.

Sam brought the heels of his hands together.

"He's a card person!" he exclaimed. "I mean, c'mon, I've seen the scissors people—they have eyes! How dumb do we think they are?"

Curtis spread his hands apart. "That's a very good point, Sam," he said.

Sam nodded. "So how do we solve this?" he asked. He crossed his arms in front of his chest.

Curtis reached into his briefcase, produced a brown paper bag, and pulled something out of it.

"This is the answer," he said. He held up a pair of black and silver scissors.

"Is that one of the scissors people?" Sam asked, recoiling a little.

"At the moment it's just a plain old pair of scissors," Curtis told him. "But tomorrow it's going to be Jack."

Sam's eyebrows pulled down close to his eyes. "How's that going to happen?"

"We're going to take Jack's code out of his card body and transfer it into these scissors . . . and then we'll add the virus . . . and the rest will be up to him."

Sam nodded slowly. "Okay, then," he said. He drew himself to his full height and looked around the room. "So I was right."

64

The next morning we were up before dawn. The brass bell of the town clock shook and clanged, and five golden globes of sound wobbled off over the rooftops of the sleeping homes. Sam and I tried to sneak down the back stairs alone, but Brinda's supersensitive ears never take a vacation, and she found us and insisted on going along. We crept outside. Across the street, a fountain splashed and rippled like a waterfall. Brinda led us through the dark streets and down to the beach. In the pale dream of dawn, the sand looked as gray as a shadow. Low in the southern sky, the last gemstones of Orion the Archer gleamed in the dusk.

Something dark and silver hurtled through the pale space of sky just above the horizon, low and fast . . . a distant jet, or something smaller and sharper? The sharp taste of fear filled my mouth.

We walked to the boat rack and lifted out the skiff. While Brinda made her rounds in the dewy beach grass, Sam took out six plastic stoppers that Curtis had brought back for us from the lab. They were designed to fit into the ends of test tubes, but with their funnel-like shape, they were also perfect for stopping up holes in a boat. I set the first one in place, and Sam raised his wooden mallet and struck a few solid blows. *Bonk. Bonk.*

"Good fit," Sam grunted.

I glanced about, worried that someone or something might have heard us.

Ever since Jack's "surgery," I had been puzzling over Dad's password. It was a darn good thing that I remembered it, but of course Dad had made sure of that, by repeating it to me several times.

"Why does Dad want to come back to life as a plum?" I asked.

"No idea, *hombre*," Sam replied. He grunted as he delivered another blow with his wooden mallet. *Bonk*.

"Did he even like plums?" I asked.

"Probably. He liked all fruit," Sam recalled. He gazed off into the distance. "Remember how much he loved starfruit and lychee?"

"Enough to want to live his life as a piece of fruit?" I placed the next stopper in position.

"Beats me."

Sam hammered away at the stopper. *Bonk. Bonk*. He raised his head and gazed for a moment at the southern sky.

"Paul, I've been wondering something." *Bonk*.

"Yes?" I replied.

"Do you really believe that Dad just disappeared? I mean, do you think the rumor might be true and he was killed?"

"I'm not sure," I replied. "But from what I know of the scissors people . . ."

Sam shuddered and held up his hand. "You don't have to say it."

I let out my breath. "Mom's the one who knows for sure, but she's not talking."

"I know." His brow wrinkled. "Has this whole thing—losing Dad, meeting the card people, fighting the scissors people—has it been good for you?"

"Good for me? How could it be good for me?"

Bonk. "I mean, have you learned anything from it?"

I was silent a minute. "Yeah. Yeah, I have." I paused a moment, trying to find the right words. "It might sound a little weird, but I've learned there's a war inside my heart," I told him.

He set down the hammer. "A war inside your heart?"

"Yeah," I replied. "A war between love and fear."

His brow wrinkled again. "What do you mean?"

"I mean, since Dad disappeared and the scissors people showed up, there's been a whole lot of fear. It can overwhelm me if I let it. The only thing that can fight it off is love. You know, thinking of Dad. Thinking of other things I love, people I love."

"Like the card people," Sam remarked.

He picked up the hammer again. *Bonk. Bonk.* He paused.

"So which is winning?" he asked.

"I don't know. They're both pretty strong."

"Yeah, they are," he agreed. He set down the hammer again. "Okay, let's try her out."

We picked up the skiff, splashed into the shallows, and lowered the boat into the water. It floated high on the waves— no sign of leaking.

"Done," Sam pronounced.

We placed the skiff on its rack and sneaked back home.

65

There were grim faces everywhere you looked—humans and card people. We were all on edge. Tonight, everything would be decided, for good or bad.

There was much to do still. The card children, led by the five remaining Clubs children, were constructing a new, larger airplane out of poster board and some balsa wood that Sam found for them in his closet. The King and Queen of Clubs hovered nearby, watching and commenting on its construction. The Queen kept sniffling and wiping tears from her eyes. "Where is the rest of our Club family?" she moaned. "Where is our Jack?"

The completed airplane had a wingspan of fully four feet and was almost six feet in length. At lunchtime, Lex, Nim, Sam and I gave it a good looking-over.

Jack hopped up onto my shoulder. "That baby's going to really move," he commented.

"You've been hanging out too much with Sam," I told him. "You're even starting to talk like him."

Sam gave Jack a high five, and Jack smiled. "Master Sam does have some colorful ways of expressing himself."

"Is this airplane going to carry you to the Haul-over tonight?" I asked.

"Oh no. No, I'm going by wind power," said Jack.

"Why the airplane, then?" Nim asked.

Jack motioned us all over closer. "It's a diversion," he confided.

"A diversion?" Lex asked.

"A false attack. To divert the attention of the scissors people."

"I get it," Sam said. "The scissors people are probably programmed to attack the high tech stuff first. So the airplane will provide cover for you."

"Exactly," Jack told him.

"But there will be real card people on the plane," Nim pointed out.

"Desperate times," Jack replied.

"That old British leader, Winston Churchill—the one who looked like a bulldog—he did something like that on D-Day, when the British landed on the French coast to drive out the Nazis," Lex said. "He set up, like, a diversionary force farther north to trick the Germans. His own son was part of it. Not a single member of that mission survived. But it allowed the real force to get through and save Europe."

"Who's going to fly the airplane?" I asked.

Jack pursed his lips. "The Queen of Clubs has volunteered to co-pilot the plane, and six of the Spades and some Diamond children are going as crew, in order to generate enough electricity. Meanwhile, all twenty-nine remaining cards will form the kite that will pull me in secret, in the dark before moonrise, across the bay to the Haul-over. Once there, I will begin my quest."

Nim looked over at the face cards. "All that royalty will be part of the kite? Even the King and the Jack of Spades? And the Jack of Diamonds?"

"Even the Ace of Clubs. Desperate times," Jack repeated. "Desperate times."

Late that afternoon, the card people stopped work and came together. As the children gathered in small groups, the face cards walked around, speaking to them softly and hugging them all, one by one.

Sam was watching them. "They really love each other," he said to me. "I mean, they really, *really* love each other."

"Curtis may have figured out how to make them think logically, but Dad was the one who gave them their hearts," I replied.

"Dad made the card people almost as good as he was."

"No one will ever be as good as Dad," I said.

Sam bent in closer. "We're still going tonight, right?" he asked.

"Yes," I replied. "I cleared it with Jack. We'll head farther down the bay and land near the jetties, so we don't interfere with Jack's arrival. Then we can sneak across the Haul-over to the cottage."

"Are Nim and Lex coming?"

"They're coming. And by the way, Mom still doesn't know we're rowing over to the Haul-over. She thinks we're staying on shore."

"It's better that way. She would worry too much," Sam agreed.

66

When Curtis came home he announced that he had completed the virus and was confident, based on his testing, that it would work. It would function much like a computer virus, by embedding itself in routine communications and then slipping out in secret to infect the scissors people. According to a recent report from the Ace of Clubs, the scissors people communicated an average of once an hour, by touching blades. At some point during this process, Jack would have to infect one or two of the scissors people with the virus, and the virus would then spread on its own from scissors to scissors.

After dinner, Curtis set up the surgery center one last time. Jack lay down on the copper strip, bumped fists with Sam and me, and allowed himself to be bound with the black elastic strips. Curtis hooked up the electrodes to him, started up the computer program, entered the three-word password, and waited for the codes to stabilize.

"All right, Jack, I've captured all your codes cleanly. In a second I'm going to cut the connection to your card body. At that time you will experience a loss of consciousness. When you come to a few minutes later, you'll be in your new body," Curtis explained.

"Yeah, I'll finally be a sharp guy," Jack quipped.

"Here we go." Curtis hit a button, and the monitor went dark. He detached the electrodes from the Jack of Hearts card and placed it carefully to the side. Then he set the silver and black scissors onto the copper strip and attached the electrodes to the tips of the blades. He brought back the computer program and watched the codes stream across the monitor until they stabilized.

"We're ready," he said. He hit a button, and the codes shimmered a second and then grew still. He hit another series of buttons to install the virus. "We're done," he announced. He detached the electrodes. "How are you feeling, Jack?" he asked.

The scissors rocked slightly back and forth.

"Jack?" I asked. "Are you there?"

"Remember," Curtis reminded me, "he won't be able to talk. He'll behave pretty much like a scissors person, without the aggression—so long as he controls his temper."

"Jack, give me some sign that you know I'm here."

The scissors rolled up on its side and looked toward me with its two dark eyes that hung suspended in the middle of the handles. One of the eyes seemed to wink, for just a second.

"It *is* you!" I exclaimed.

Jack tried to stand up, but immediately clattered back onto the slate. He tried again, and this time he was able to hobble forward a few steps on his two points before he slipped and fell.

"Jack, would it be easier to learn how to walk on the carpet?" I asked. The eye winked.

I carried Jack into the living room and set him on the rug. Jack hopped up onto the points of his blades and looked around at us all, turning his entire body from side to side. His eyes wiggled slightly.

The children pulled back against the sofa.

"He looks scary," the Five of Diamonds mumbled.

"Are we sure he isn't a bad guy?" the Four of Clubs asked.

"Don't be silly—that's our dear little Jack of Hearts!" the Queen of Hearts assured them. "Can't you tell?"

"No," they both said, drawing back further.

Then, with the stiff-legged gait of a cowboy who has been too long in the saddle, Jack lurched across the rug toward them. He stopped a few feet in front of them, winked, and collapsed helplessly onto the rug. The card children laughed. But he was quickly back on his feet and trundling across the rug in the other direction. When he came back to his original starting point, he was able to pivot on one leg without falling and start again. Already his walk was growing smoother and more graceful.

Curtis nodded in appreciation from the doorway. "That's much better, Jack. You'll need to advance rapidly to the next level. The scissors people will sense any hesitancy in your movements."

Jack stopped and looked toward Curtis, and something about his eyes seemed to glimmer.

An hour later, Jack was able to walk even on slippery surfaces like wood. He could also lift himself a few inches into the air, but he was unable to fly.

"Don't worry about the flying part," Curtis said. "That will come in time—perhaps sooner than you think. The scissors people make use of their super-magnetic qualities to achieve flight—quite ingenious, actually."

Fingers entwined, Nim and Lex sat side by side on the floor, watching Jack's progress. Once when I glanced over at Lex, our eyes met and held. Awkward.

Later that evening, as I was washing some dinner dishes, Lex appeared beside me.

"Hey, uh, I was wondering, dude, are you, like, okay about Nim and me?" he asked.

"Of course," I replied quickly. "I'm fine." I could feel the blood rushing to my face.

"I mean, because I asked Nim about you and her before all this happened, and she said you were, like, just friends."

"That's right. We're friends. We've been friends since she came to America."

"'Cause, you know, I never meant to be in the middle of anything, you know what I'm saying?"

"Yeah, I know. It's fine."

"I like you, dude. I mean, you're a pretty quiet guy and all, but you know what they say, still waters run deep."

"Yeah. Thanks."

"Then we're cool." And Lex bumped fists with me and walked away.

Later, Nim caught up to me in the hallway. "Did Lex talk with you?"

I nodded.

"I told him you were fine with everything, but he keeps thinking you're having a problem with us," she explained.

"There's no problem," I said, miserably.

"He's a great guy, isn't he?" When her eyes filled with light, she looked so pretty. Her black hair glistened like the night sky.

"Yeah . . . great," I heard myself say.

"Thanks, Paul. You're the best." And then she bent in closer, pressing softly against me with the front of her blouse, and gave me a quick kiss on the cheek. She smelled like spring and flowers, and the kiss remained on my cheek for a minute or two.

67

It was time.

The card people and the humans had one last meeting. Jack, who normally spoke on behalf of his King and Queen, stood silently to the side on his gleaming scissors legs, while the King and Queen of Hearts stepped forward on the coffee table and gestured for everyone's attention.

"Since the first dawning of our consciousness, we have searched for our mission. That mission is now clear to us," the King intoned, slowly but grandly.

"It is indeed," the Queen proclaimed. "Our mission is to stop the brutal force of the scissors people before they can wreak destruction on an innocent world."

She then laid out the details of timing and execution. The key point, she emphasized, was that the airplane must fly across the bay just ahead of the kite that would be towing Jack. That would give Jack cover, so he could arrive undetected on the shore, where he would then make his way secretly into the midst of the scissors people. The Queen of Clubs stood and turned to Curtis.

"Will the scissors people be at full strength?" she asked. "Have they regained all their power?"

"By now, I believe they have more than regained their full power," Curtis replied. "I anticipate that their force will, in fact, be overwhelming."

"That there is danger, let none of us doubt," the King of Hearts acknowledged. "But we face it with a glad heart, knowing the cause for which we fight."

"There are those of us who stand ready to lay down our own lives in the service of a fair lady," the Jack of Diamonds announced, with a glance toward Nim.

The King of Spades, the King of Diamonds, and the King of Clubs promenaded to the front to stand beside their fellow King. The three Queens came up beside them. The card people bowed their heads, and we humans did as well.

"Let us go bravely and without fear," intoned the King of Spades.

The Queen of Clubs concluded, "And may our hearts be full of love, love for one another and for our human friends."

"And let's kick those scissors people's butts!" Sam exclaimed.

There was a tiny roar of approval, and the card people lifted their heads and began to stir about. Sam gave me the thumbs-up sign. It was time.

68

Before he took on his scissors body, Jack had asked Nim—"So there's no confusion for you humans, either"—to write the following on a piece of posterboard which was set on a table in the living room:

Kite:

Two, Three, Four, Six, and Nine of Clubs

Two, Three, Five, Six, Eight, Nine, and Ten of Hearts

Three, Four, Nine, and Ten of Spades

Two, Three, Four, Ten of Diamonds

King of Hearts

King and Ace of Clubs

Jack, Queen, King of Diamonds, Jack and King of Spades

Queen of Hearts (captain)

Jack of Hearts (passenger)

Airplane:

Five, Seven, and Nine of Diamonds

Six, Seven, and Eight of Spades

Queen of Clubs

At the bottom Nim had scrawled: "I hold each of you in my heart."

69

In the next few minutes, the card people sorted themselves into the two groups. The airplane people hopped up the stairs to the second floor and threaded their way up the ship's ladder to the tower, where they exited through the trap door and onto the flat section of roof beside the tower. This was to be their launching pad for their flight. Here they would wait until they received word that the kite people stood ready at the water's edge.

We said good-bye to Mom. "You'll be back soon?" she asked.

"Yeah, Mom, soon," I told her. Her eyes lingered on me, but she said nothing more. She might have sensed that we had different meanings of the word *soon*.

While Curtis and Mom stayed home to maintain a base of operations, we kids walked the kite people to the shore. I had the cards stowed away in my shirt pocket, and Nim carried Jack the scissors man, along with a plastic bag. Sam brought the extra supplies, and Lex was again donating his kazoo. We made our way quickly and silently out the back door and onto the street. As always, Brinda nosed along ahead of us.

In the hour after sunset, a misty haze covered the town like the cap of a mushroom. Footsteps and voices sounded muffled and dull, as if you heard them through cotton. Our breath floated in front of us in little clouds. As we came closer to the shore, the mist thickened into silver droplets of water that stuck to our cheeks and our clothes.

At the water's edge the card people got to work, binding themselves together with the lines of thread. Nim zipped Jack into the plastic bag and tied him with stout yarn to one side of the kazoo. Triple lines of thread lashed the kazoo to the kite. In a few minutes' time, all was ready. The kazoo bobbed at the water's edge.

Nim was on her cell phone, calling Mom. "We're ready," she told Mom. "They are? The plane just launched? Okay." She turned to shore and gave the thumbs up signal.

The Queen of Hearts climbed onto the platform to prepare to steer her little ship across the bay, the card people spaced themselves out along the shoreline, and at a signal from the King of Hearts, they all leaped into the air, led by the Ace of Clubs. Using the skill and grace that came from hours of practice, they caught the wind and held steady. The Queen of Hearts pushed off with her stirring stick, and with a smooth ripple and a hollow bubbling sound, the kazoo slid away from shore.

The card kite melted into the mist.

70

Sam and I lifted the boat off the rack and carried it into the shallows. Once the rest of us were on board, he pushed the skiff into deeper water. He hopped over the side and was soon pulling vigorously at the oars. Brinda lay near him on the floor-boards.

We were about halfway across the bay when a gray shape sailed overhead in the haze.

"That was the plane," I said.

"I saw the Queen of Clubs in front, piloting it," Nim declared.

"No way," Lex told her. "I could barely see anything."

"Your eyes are old," she teased him. She squeezed his hand and gazed upwards. "Best wishes to our aviators."

Sam rowed on, turning his head now and then to glance forward. He was bringing us down the bay toward the jetties, a mile or so from the spot where Jack would be landing.

A few minutes later Nim stood up in the bow. "There's something floating up ahead," she said. "Steer to the right a little," she called softly to Sam.

A minute later Lex reached out over the gunwale and dragged something out of the water. He shook it and set it on the seat.

It was the waterlogged tail of the airplane.

"Oh no," Nim moaned.

"Oh man," Lex said.

"Look around, everyone! There might be survivors!" Nim exclaimed.

For the next several minutes we rowed back and forth across the area, but all we found was a few more pieces of balsa wood.

There were no signs of card people anywhere.

"Seven more lost," Nim moaned. She buried her head on Lex's shoulder.

Sam rowed on, tears streaming down his face.

We pressed on into the veil of mist.

71

About ten minutes later Sam brought the boat up onto the beach, and we hopped out and dragged it above the tide line.

"How are we getting there?" Lex asked. "Can we walk along the beach?"

"No," I told him. "Too exposed." I explained that we would bushwhack through the brush and try to intercept the road.

It was difficult going. The vegetation was dense—bayberry bushes that caught you with their branches, beach plum with little rough nubs, scratchy scrub oak. Sam picked up Brinda and carried her so she wouldn't get lost. In the darkness and fog, it was almost impossible to know where to go.

Finally we stumbled into a cleared area.

Sam bent down for a better look. "It's the road!" he exclaimed. "See, the sand is softer, and there's a line of grass down the middle!"

"Thank goodness," Nim said.

She moved into the lead, with Lex beside her. Sam and I brought up the rear.

As the wind started to rise, the fog and mist began to break apart. Wisps of clouds drifted about, silvery gray in the light of the half moon.

We pressed on. We climbed over one hill and descended into a cooler, damper valley where a few pockets of fog lay thick as cream. We climbed another, larger hill, and the mist fell away. Here Nim stopped, and we all came up beside her.

"I can see the house!" she said softly.

"Yeah, that's it," Sam said. "And there's some scissors people on the lawn."

"No way you can see them," I replied.

"Yes way. I see 'em there," Sam insisted.

"Let's get closer." I led the way now. We came around a little bend and stopped under a pine tree. We were no more than thirty yards from the lawn in front of the house.

"See? I told you," Sam whispered, in the tiniest voice he could muster.

The scissors people had gathered there—a huge swarm of them—it must have been a hundred or more. They were bouncing around on the grass, almost like a football team before a big game, and slamming into each other with their black handles.

"That's freaky," Lex murmured.

"Even scissors people have rituals," Sam marveled. He set down Brinda beside him and told her to be still.

"It might be the way they make sure everyone is loyal," I suggested.

"I hope Jack is fitting in," Nim said.

"He's smart, he'll know what to do," Lex assured her.

The scissors people began to sort themselves out across the grass. It looked like they were creating a shape of some sort. Two groups, nearer the house, had formed two circles right next to each other. Another group, closer to the water, made two lines that met where the circles touched.

"What are they doing?" Sam asked.

"I don't know," Nim replied.

"Picture it from above," I said quietly. "Don't you see?"

"No," Sam replied.

"They're forming a giant pair of scissors."

"OMG. You're right!" Nim breathed.

"It's like they worship the great god of scissors," Lex observed.

72

One of the scissors people looked out of place. It tried to join one of the straight lines, but there was no room. It skittered over to one of the circles, but found itself blocked out there, too. It tried to squeeze into the place where the lines met, but that spot was already occupied.

The entire outline had been created, and the extra pair of scissors was left there, standing alone, in the open space between the two blades.

The last shreds of clouds pulled apart in the freshening breeze, and the moon came out brighter. All the scissors were standing at attention, completely silent and still, and a hundred pairs of small black eyes watched the leftover in the middle.

"Do something, Jack," Sam whispered. "You can't just stand there!"

The scissors in the middle took a few steps to the left, then back to the right. I thought I saw its eyes glimmering faintly in confusion.

"Here's your big test," Lex whispered.

"Come on, Jack," I murmured. "Think of something, anything that will impress them."

Then the scissors started moving. It executed a perfect spin move on one point and took a step forward on the other. It stepped back, leaned left, leaned right, stepped left, then right. It repeated the routine. It leaped up into the air and fell to the ground, legs spread in a perfect split. Then it sprung up again.

"He's dancing!" Nim exclaimed.

"It's the Temptations' moves!" Sam told them.

The dancing grew faster, more intense: multiple spins, several scissors kicks, a succession of hops, more splits and flips, spin moves upside down on its head, bounces on its side off the ground . . .

"What are the other scissors doing?" Sam asked.

The scissors people had been watching silently and without motion, but now they started to shake. Some of them were actually leaning back and forth like tiny trees swaying in the breeze.

"They're scared," Sam guessed.

"They're angry," Lex conjectured.

"They're laughing!" Nim declared. "Look—don't you see it?—they're laughing!"

It did look like laughter, but not nice laughter. It was like the cruel, heartless laughter of gulls when they come upon a group of defenseless clams.

"I think he won them over," Sam said hopefully.

"I don't think they're the type who get won over," I whispered.

Three of the scissors were approaching Jack. They surrounded him and then, as one, they slammed into him with their handles, knocking him onto the ground. They began body-slamming him, one after the other.

"Ow!" Sam exclaimed.

"Come on, Jack, don't let them keep you down," I urged, under my breath.

Almost before the words were out of my mouth, Jack was up and on his feet again. He slammed into the others with his handles, they slammed back. They all started revolving, slamming handles like cogs of a gear . . . and then, somehow, they disengaged, and Jack was hopping over with the others back to one of the circles, where he found a place waiting for him.

"Initiation!" Nim said.

"Well done, Jack!" Sam declared. "But now what?"

What happened next left us speechless. The closest human parallel I could think of was another sports comparison: a pre-game ritual by a basketball team, the sort of thing where each member of the starting five takes a turn running the gauntlet of his teammates. But here, instead of five teammates, it was a hundred, and instead of slapping five or bumping fists, the interaction was harsh and brutal.

Starting with the circle on the right, the scissors took turns, one by one, making their way around the entire inside perimeter of their formation, slamming into each and every scissors they met. They struck one another handle to handle, so loud and hard that the noise carried to us like a sledgehammer pounding on steel. Any pair of scissors that lost its footing was immediately body-slammed by the ones around it and tried desperately to bounce back to its feet.

The ritual had gone on for several minutes, and Jack was still waiting for his turn.

"If he touches their handles, will he transfer the virus to them?" Nim whispered to me. The wind had come up again, and branches rattled beside us.

"I think Curtis said he has to touch them blade-to-blade," I replied.

"He'll figure out a way!" Sam exclaimed, pounding his fists together. "C'mon, Jack!"

Then it was Jack's turn.

He hopped into the middle of his circle, did a scissors split as if in sheer exuberance, and rose parallel to the ground, hovering on his side a few inches above the grass. Then, like a basketball player giving low fives to his teammates, he floated around the first circle, touching each blade he met.

"It's working!" Sam whispered.

"I'm not sure they like this," I whispered back.

"I don't see how you can tell," Sam came back.

It seemed to be going all right . . . until Jack came to the start of the second circle. There, three scissors people stepped out in front of him, stopped him, and slammed him down. One by one, they hopped on top of him and pounded him, again and again, driving him into the ground. Their handles whirled like egg-beaters of unimaginable strength and speed.

"No!" we exclaimed.

There was a sound like a steel bar being put through a blender.

"They're going to kill him!" Nim cried. "Stop it!"

"Nim." Lex tried to calm her.

She stood up. "Let him go! I mean it!"

Suddenly she tore off down the path, ran up onto the lawn . . . and came to a stop a few yards in front of them.

73

At that moment, everything seemed to change. The wind, which for some time had been gaining strength, died away to nothing. The moon shone with greater intensity and brilliance, as if focusing on the scene on the lawn. The cries of gulls faded away in the distance.

Like a swarm of bees, the scissors people—all but a few from the first circle—rose swiftly into the air. They flew forward and formed a dense line of attack, with their points aimed at Nim. Their blades glinted in the moonlight and their eyes dangled like dark jewels in the middle of their black handles.

"Come back, Nim!" Lex called to her. "Come back here before it's too late!"

But Nim was frozen. She stood by herself at the edge of the lawn, facing the scissors people. Her only motion was the clenching and unclenching of her fingers.

I couldn't see her face, but I could imagine the fear and the bravery that were dancing in her eyes as she faced this danger alone. At that instant, somewhere inside me, I felt something let go, like a ripe fruit falling free.

The line of scissors floated closer to her with the deadly, menacing calm of a tiger preparing to spring.

My next thoughts didn't come to me in words, but as a picture fully formed.

I bent down, grabbed two handfuls of sand, and took off. I raced down the path, so fast I felt no weight or resistance. My feet left the soft sand of the road and pounded up onto the packed earth of the lawn. Before I knew how it happened, I was beside Nim, then moving out in front of her.

"What do you think you're doing, Paul?" she asked fiercely.

"What does it look like?" I replied, every bit as fiercely.

"I can take care of myself."

"I know that."

But I also knew that this was really my fight, not hers.

74

The scissors people floated closer to us and stopped, poised a few yards above the ground, less than ten feet from us.

Somewhere above us, I could feel the stars, or something like the stars, glinting in the darkness, and for some reason I thought of the peaceful drift of leafy fireflies on a perfect summer night.

There was a sudden, brighter glint along the line of the scissors people, like a smile flashing across an evil face.

No time to spare.

I tossed the handfuls of sand into the air, turned, and pushed Nim to the ground. Then I fell across her, shielding her from above. As I fell, I caught a glimpse of the scissors rushing above us toward the decoy of the sand. But I knew it wouldn't fool them for long.

My body tensed for what I knew was coming.

As the grains of sand rained down on us, I said my goodbyes to Mom, to Sam, to Dad, to the world.

But what came next was not at all what I expected.

I became aware of a vast chattering, an outburst of song, like the cries of countless birds; I heard the faint clank somewhere of metal on metal; I could swear I even heard a silver melody as pale and fragile as moonlight.

Was this death?

If so, it must be heaven, because it smelled like sunshine and roses.

75

"Get off of me, will you!" Nim yelled. Her voice was muffled by dirt and grass. "Get off me!"

My face had been in her hair.

She pushed me roughly to the side, and we both sat up. I'm not sure which of us was more dazed and confused. She wiped the dirt from her face and glanced around.

What was this? What had happened?

All around us on the ground lay scores of scissors people, rolling about like baby seals, clinking handles in a gentle, friendly way.

In and among them strolled the card people, bumping fists, talking and smiling and, some of them, crying.

And at the heart of it all, on his stiff metal legs, his eyes winking with pleasure, walked . . . Jack, with a sprightly air that was unmistakable, even in his guise as a scissors person.

Brinda trotted up, sniffed at Jack, and wagged her tail.

I held out my arms, and Jack ran up and hopped, landing safely on his side in my arms.

"You did it!" I exclaimed.

Jack's eyes shimmered, just for a moment.

Then Sam was beside us.

"Are you okay?" he asked.

"I'm fine," I replied.

"You sure?"

"I'm sure."

"That was awesome!" Sam exclaimed. "So awesome! Did you see what happened?"

"Not really," I replied. Suddenly I felt very tired.

"Somehow—don't ask me how, because I don't know—Jack dug his way out of the ground. Then he flew up into the air and touched blades with them all, which gave them the virus. It was all at the very last second! It was amazing! He is such a hero!" Sam called out for the world to hear.

Jack rolled over in my arms, the way Brinda does when she wants her belly to be scratched.

"You're a great guy, Jack!" I told him, patting him on the top of his handles.

Several yards away, Lex was hugging Nim. She looked as if she had been crying. She pulled away from him then and turned toward me. I could feel her eyes searching for mine.

"What about David Westfield?" I asked. Cupping Jack in my palms—somehow it didn't feel right to let him perch on my shoulder as usual—I stood and peered over toward the house. Just as I thought, there they were. In the ghostly glow of moonlight, I could see the outlines of four people standing in the driveway, peering back at us.

Jack's eyes shimmered with a yellow light.

"No, Jack," I told him. "You're not allowed to kill humans. No matter what."

Jack turned to me and winked. He leaped out of my hands and soared off through the air toward the house. A few yards short of David and the others, he stopped in the air, turned, and hovered, pointing at the humans with the tips of his blades.

There was a scream, and David and Julie hopped into one car and the other two men jumped into the pickup truck and then, with a wild scattering of gravel and sand, they were gone, down the sandy road, followed close behind by a single pair of flying scissors.

"Yee haw! You go, Jack!" Sam yelled, running halfway across the lawn. "Don't let 'em get away! Yee haw!"

76

Nim walked over to me. She slipped a strand of her hair behind her ear. "I still have my phone. Should I call someone?" she asked. She seemed sad and quiet.

For a moment the world went black, then slowly recovered in shades of gray and silver. "Yeah. Call Mom—she'll alert the police," I said.

Nim stepped off to the side and made the call. She came back to me and stopped very near. Her voice was soft and close. "Your mother sounded pretty upset that we're over here. I told her we're all fine, and she seemed to settle down. She's already calling the police. She thinks they'll form a roadblock and get those guys."

"Good," I replied. I looked shyly toward her, then away.

"Paul, you were going to give up your life to save mine," she said. Her voice was packed solid with intensity, almost like anger or an accusation, but it was something a lot nicer than that.

She was gazing right at me, waiting for me to respond.

"That's right," I said, glancing at her and holding her eye.

"Why?" she asked, in a voice full of sorrow.

A surge of emotion started to lift the words from me like a wave lifting a swimmer into the sky.

"Because I . . ." I began. Then, somehow, at the last moment, I pulled back. The wave broke and fell beneath me. "You would do the same for me," I told her, with a small shrug.

"Because we've been friends so long," she said, more like a question than a statement.

"Yes," I said.

She put her arms around me and hugged me so tight, I wondered if all the breath and life were being squeezed out of me.

"You're a liar, and I love you for it," she whispered in my ear in a low, thrilling voice, and then she kissed me tenderly, sweetly on the lips and staggered away across the sandy grass.

77

Dad and I were sitting at the table in the living room, playing cards. All the cards were alive and participating in the game. My suit of choice had always been Clubs, and the Ten of Clubs was especially helpful on this night, grinning at me mischievously and doing slick tricks like forming an inside straight when I needed it.

Jack was also helpful, creating a royal flush for me with the Hearts royal family. Despite all the extra help I was receiving, Dad still managed to win more than he lost, as usual. He was eating his favorite dessert snack, gulab jamun, and he offered me some of the sweet balls of fried milk dough, soaked in cardamom.

Now and then Dad stopped his play to make a brief, witty observation. But toward the end of the game he pushed back his chair and began to talk more at length and with greater seriousness.

"When you stepped in front of her, that was a brave and fine thing. But do you know what was even finer?"

"What?" I asked.

"When she asked you why you did it, and you didn't declare your love."

"I don't see what was so great about that."

Dad smoothed back his thinning dark hair. "Of course you do. It would have put her in an impossible situation. It would have forced her into a choice that she can't make at this time."

"I was just confused and afraid, Dad."

"For good reason. Your confusion and fear were signs that the time was not right."

"I don't know what you mean."

Dad smiled. "You're like a puppy with large feet, Paul. When great dogs are small puppies, they're forever stumbling over their feet until they've had a chance to grow into them. The confusion you feel now is a sign of the greatness that may come to you one day. Like one of those puppies, you still need to grow into yourself. You've already done a lot of growing, these past few days."

"Dad, can I ask you something?"

"Ask away." Dad dealt out the cards again. The Ten of Clubs slid out of the deck, tiptoed across the table, and hopped into my hand.

"Why do you want to come back to life as a plum?" I asked.

Dad's smile stretched wider.

"What makes you think it's a choice?" he replied, playing a card.

"What does that mean?"

Dad set his cards down on the table and looked me full in the face. His brown eyes glimmered softly. "Look, Paul, sometime—years in the future—when you and Nim are finally all grown up and ready . . ."

"What are you talking about?"

Dad shrugged. "Sorry, that just slipped out."

"Dad, I don't know what's wrong with me. I don't feel very good."

Dad leaned over toward me, his eyes glowing as they always did when he was happy, and he put his hand on mine.

"I'm sorry for all this, son. I have no doubt that you'll understand one day. In all of this great world, with all its many wonders, it's the greatest gift that anyone can ever hope to . . ."

He shuddered and turned to me. His eyes opened a touch wider, and then, as I watched in horror, the light drained out of them. He collapsed forward onto the table.

Protruding from Dad's chest were the black handles of a pair of scissors. The malicious eyes wriggled ever so slightly, looking at me in cruel, mocking triumph.

78

I woke up drenched in sweat. Mom was standing by the bed. A few yards away, Brinda slept peacefully on the floor.

"Are you okay, darling?" Mom asked. "You were screaming in your sleep."

"I'm fine." But I knew I wasn't. I felt weak and feverish, and a gray shadow lay between me and the world of the living.

It came back to me then, the events of the previous night. Jack's heroism. The capture of the two men in the pickup truck. The maddening escape, against all reason, of David Westfield and Julie down back roads that the police, somehow, hadn't been able to cover.

"Mom," I said on a sudden impulse, "tell me the truth about Dad. He's dead, isn't he?"

Mom sat down on the bed, reached over, and smoothed back my hair.

"Is this really a good time to talk?" she asked.

"I just had a dream. Maybe it was only a nightmare. Or maybe not. I need to know the truth."

Mom sighed.

"I knew one day we'd come to this," she murmured.

I asked her with my eyes to go on. She sighed again. She took my right hand and held it to her face, kissed it, and pressed it between her hands.

"Okay," she began.

"Your father was in a car accident," she said. "It was on Memorial Drive as he was coming back home from MIT that night. The car had lurched out of control. It came to a stop beside the road."

"So he was dead, and that rumor was true. And you've known it all along," I breathed. "Why didn't you tell me?"

"Your father had warned me that something might happen . . . but he begged me, whatever it was, to tell you and Sam simply that he had disappeared."

The walls of my room were melting, they were starting to stream about in waves of colorless motion. "Why, Mom?"

"I don't know. I really don't know."

"What good did it do to keep this from us?"

"I don't know that either."

I willed the world around me to stop moving. "Is that all there is to tell?"

"No, there's more." Mom tried to say something else, but tears welled up in her eyes, and she turned her head aside.

"You mean it was more than just a car accident?" I watched her closely.

"Yes," she replied quietly. She took out a tissue and dabbed at her eyes. "Oh," she said, shaking her head. "I never wanted to have to talk to you about all this."

79

"Mom, I've heard the ugly rumor already."

"Well, it's true," she said, taking a deep breath. "Your father's body had been pierced through by something very sharp in about . . . fifty places, and he had already lost consciousness even before the accident." Her voice broke up with the last few words. She put her head down in her hands. "The examiner couldn't believe it when he saw the body. The FBI and the university hushed everything up and told me to keep it quiet," she said, through her hands.

I reached out and put my hand on her forearm. "You should have told me," I groaned. My breath was growing shorter, and my hand started to shake.

"I couldn't, Paul. Someone from the CIA visited me after the accident and ordered me to maintain strict silence about it—or face federal charges. The order was signed by the President himself. It was national security. They said something about it being the first murder of a human by nanotechnology. Which I guess it was, and I pray to God that it will be the last," she said, looking over at me. There was something honest and direct in her eyes that I hadn't seen in a long time.

"Then why are you telling me now?"

"Tonight I received a call from the President. He had heard about everything you kids had done. He praised your heroism, and he said you deserved to know."

"So that's it . . . Dad's really dead?" I asked.

"Yes," she said. I leaned my head against hers. We both wept.

Finally, after several minutes, I sat up again.

"That means the scissors people were already at full force back then," I pointed out.

"Only for a short while," she replied. "Curtis thinks that single effort cost the scissors people weeks of recovery time, and that was what gave the card people a chance to get established." She fished a tissue out of her bag.

"So when did Dad sprinkle the nanodust on the cards?" I asked.

Mom pursed her mouth. "I've tried to figure that out. I think he must have done it on his last morning, the day of the accident," she said. "He slipped off into the living room before he left for work that day. At the time I didn't know why."

"You knew he was in danger."

"He had feared for his life for weeks. He had been working so desperately on the nanodust. But I didn't realize that he had succeeded."

She straightened out the covers over me. "You've done some pretty amazing things of your own, Paul. Dad would be so proud of you."

Suddenly I felt very tired. "Where are the card people?"

"They're just coming out now," Mom told me.

Like flowers, I found myself thinking. Like flowers blooming. My thoughts themselves were flowers now, heavy-petaled daisies and lilies, nodding and swaying in a breeze from some distant shore . . . somewhere across the ocean where waters still rose and fell in peace.

As I drifted back to sleep, I caught a glimpse of the card people walking around on the bed. A number of the children in all the families, nine face cards and an Ace. If eyes could be trusted, most, maybe all, of the twenty-nine card people still remained.

"Where's Jack?" I heard myself asking as if from another dimension.

"He's here. Tonight Curtis is going to put him back in his card body. Sleep tight, darling."

"You have to tell Sam," I murmured, and then a dark curtain closed in front of my vision and sleep, thick velvet sleep, flowed over me.

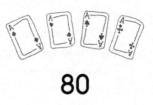

80

Around noon I woke up again. I was still tired, but the feverish aching was gone. A pair of scissors hopped up on the bed and lay down next to me like a cat.

"Still a scissors person, huh?" I asked Jack, patting him on top of the handles. "Well, from what I hear, Curtis will get you back in your own body pretty soon." Jack's eyes twinkled.

Sam came in shortly afterwards. "Mom told me," he said in a very still voice. I gave Sam a hug and tried to say something reassuring, but the words wouldn't come out. He got up and found a box of tissues for us both. Neither of us said much for a while.

When we began to talk, we caught up on the events of the past few days, including David Westfield's escape and what it might mean. We both were worried that Westfield had more of his nanodust stashed away somewhere—the primitive version that he had used for the scissors people.

"He's not going to sprinkle it on something as simple as scissors next time," Sam declared. "He'll put it on guns, or jet bombers, or something like that."

"Yeah, I know."

"Even those scissors could have been terrible, once they reached full power—no telling what awful things they might have done," Sam said.

"Thanks to Jack for stopping them," I replied, patting the scissors again. "Oh, and Jack, once you get your normal shape back, I hope we can hear the full details of what it was like being among those scissors people."

There was a slight motion next to me on the bed.

"He's trembling," Sam observed. "Poor guy."

I picked Jack up and petted him softly. "You don't have to talk about it unless you want to," I said.

Sam watched in silence for a minute.

"Hey, did you ever find out anything about the flashing light you saw in the camera of your laptop?" he asked.

"It had to be Westfield. I'm pretty sure he found a way to break into my computer and track us."

"I don't know, I don't think it was him," Sam contended.

"Who else could it've been?"

"I think it's the CIA," Sam said, leaning in closer and talking more softly.

"The CIA? Why?"

"They knew about Dad's death, they knew about nanotechnology. They were tracking us."

A shiver ran down my spine. I felt suddenly exhausted. "I think I need to sleep some more," I told him.

81

When I woke up again late that afternoon, Sam was sitting at my desk, playing a video game on his phone. He grunted at me but didn't look up.

A few minutes later there was a soft knock on the door, and Nim appeared in the doorway, paused, and took a few hesitant steps into the room. She glanced around at the walls of my bedroom as if she didn't quite recognize them.

"What's the matter with you?" Sam asked.

"Nothing!" she replied, reaching for his belly and tickling him.

"Ew, a girl! Get away from me!" Sam exclaimed. He fell to the floor, doubled over in laughter. He'd always been completely helpless against tickling.

Nim tickled him some more and then asked, "Sam, could I have a minute alone with Paul?"

"Well, I guess I know when I'm not wanted," Sam declared, and he left the room with a large smirk on his face.

"Hey, Paul," Nim said.

"How you doin'?" I asked.

"Okay," she replied, slipping her feet out of her shoes and arching her soles. She came over, folded her legs under her, and sat on the bed a few feet from me.

"What's up?" I asked.

"Umm . . . Lex and I sort of had a fight," she said.

"Oh. Sorry."

"Yeah. Because of that kiss I gave you."

"Oh, don't worry about that." I waved a hand in front of my face.

"I think I got carried away by the moment," she said.

"Yeah, hey, you know, it didn't change anything."

She sought my eyes with hers and found them. For a minute, her eyes darted back and forth, from my right eye to my left eye and back again. I knew she was looking for something, and I knew, at least for now, that I could hold my feelings just far enough inside so she couldn't see.

But her face was so nice to look upon, and her eyes had that special kind of amber light in them that I'd never seen anywhere else.

"So we're just friends, right?" she asked.

"Yeah," I told her. "Good old friends."

"Really good old friends," she agreed, "the best friends ever," and she bent over and kissed me on the cheek. Again, the kiss seemed to linger there longer than was humanly possible.

"So you won't feel weird around Lex?" she asked. "It's all good," I replied. "He's . . . he's . . ."

"He's a good guy," she finished for me.

"Yeah." I nodded.

"That's true." She frowned. "But . . . I don't know . . . sometimes we have problems. He wants . . ."

I held up my hands. "Not my business," I told her.

She glanced at me. "Sorry. I guess I have to work out my boyfriend problems on my own. My mom doesn't think I should start dating till I'm eighteen. And then she thinks I should marry the first person I ever date. That's what she did with my dad." She flipped back her dark, lustrous hair. "Isn't that like too weird for words?"

"That's parents for you," I told her.

There was a knock on the door.

"Can I come in yet?" Sam asked. He had a mischievous little grin on his face.

"Come on in," Nim replied. "But I might tickle you again if you're not good."

82

"Hopefully, this is the last time we'll have to strap you down on the operating table," Curtis told Jack later that evening as he set the elastic bands in place.

In silence, with Mom and me watching, Curtis reversed the earlier procedure. He collected the code from the scissors and stored it on the computer, set the now-lifeless scissors aside, and positioned the card carefully on the metal surgery table.

"A question for you both," he said to Mom and me, as he hooked the electrodes up to the card.

"Yes?" I asked.

He glanced at Mom, then at me. "Do I put Samir's restraint codes back in place, or do I leave them off, which means essentially that Jack will be as he was when you were training him how to control his aggressive impulses?"

"Wow," I said. "That's a pretty big question, isn't it?"

"It is," Curtis agreed.

"I don't know. I guess he might have more freedom if we leave off the restraints."

"Put him back the way Samir designed him," Mom said firmly. "We have to honor the work of my husband."

Curtis frowned slightly. "But Samir himself, if he were here today, might want to give Jack the chance to make his own decisions about his various impulses."

"Put him back as he was," Mom reiterated. "I insist. Everything else is too risky."

Curtis looked at me and shrugged. "I guess that settles it," he said, with the slightest hint of a smile on his face.

He copied the codes onto the card. Jack's eyes opened, and he raised his head and looked around. "Hey, Doc, heart still good?" he joked.

"Better than ever. One more minute, Jack, I'm giving you back your restraint codes."

"I was hoping you would," Jack said. "It's far too much work controlling your impulses all day—I don't know how you humans do it. Waste of time and effort, in my humble opinion. Now what's that I see up there? Is another incredibly annoying moth there again?"

"Yo, Jack, try to keep away from the aggressive center, will you?" Sam called to him from the doorway.

Curtis made a few more keystrokes. "You're done!" he announced, unhooking the electrodes. "And please allow me to be the first to thank you for the extraordinary act of heroism that you performed last night."

"It was my job and my pleasure," Jack said politely. He stood up and stretched. He shook his legs and wiggled his arms. "Oh, it feels so good to be flexible again," he announced. "Now where's my favorite spot?"

He ran over to me, hopped up onto my shoulder, and rubbed his head against my neck.

"It's nice to say hello," he mumbled contentedly. "But I hope you'll understand that I need to be with my people now."

"Of course. They're in the living room," I told him.

Jack spent the next few hours with the other card people. All the cards on the kite had survived, and thirty card people still remained, despite all the dangers and disasters of the past few days. Their reunion with Jack was joyous. The sound of their voices mingled like the stirrings of summer leaves.

Later, the card people joined hands, stood in a circle, and conducted a service in memory of the brave cards who had flown the diversionary airplane across the bay. One by one, they said aloud the names of the seven card people whom they had lost.

"Our young style-setters and philosophers will be sorely missed, as will our intrepid Queen," the King of Hearts concluded sadly. "But they gave their lives in the service of the greatest good. And those of us who remain represent all ages and all families of the card people—affording us new opportunities, through good deeds, to honor those whom we lost."

After the service, the card people mingled with us again. I asked about the lights in the sky that I saw just before I tossed the sand into the air.

"Yes, that was us," the Jack of Spades confirmed, twirling his black moustache. "We had been flying about in place, secured by a line to a tree, waiting to see if we might help somehow. Thank goodness it turned out as it did."

Curtis had a bit of information about the two men who had been captured. According to the police, they denied any knowledge of David Westfield's scientific projects, and they also denied any involvement in Mom's accident. But one of them apparently was overheard in the jailhouse cafeteria making a remark to the other that the real object of that attack had been Curtis, and each of them blamed the other for the mess-up.

83

Later that evening, Sam asked Jack again if he could tell us anything about his experience with the scissors people. Jack shuddered and was silent for a few long minutes before he spoke.

"It was awful," he said finally. He shook his head and was silent again.

"What was the most awful thing?" Sam gently asked.

"How cruel they were. How unspeakably cruel."

"In what way?"

"In all ways," Jack replied. He seemed to be gaining strength now. "Their greatest pleasure is to see living things suffer. They spend all their time insulting each other and laughing at each other and at everything else you can imagine."

"Are you saying that the scissors people can talk?" Curtis asked. "Do they have a language of some sort?"

"Yes, in a way, but it's silent," Jack explained. "It's visible . . . sort of like a shadow that forms different images. I don't really know if I can explain it properly."

"What are the insults like?" Curtis questioned.

"Gross comments. They like to tell each other that they smell like human body parts, things like that. I won't go into the details."

"Yuck," Sam said.

Nim had been listening in silence. "May I ask you a question, Jack?"

"You may indeed," he replied politely.

"Why did you perform your dance for them?" she asked.

"Oh, the dance? That was the inspiration of the moment."

"Dance?" Mom asked.

"Jack entertained the other scissors people with a dance," I explained. "I think he sort of won them over with it."

"He used all the Temptations' moves I taught him," Sam explained proudly.

Curtis was watching with interest. "Did you really charm them with a dance?" he asked.

"Well, that wasn't exactly how it happened," Jack explained.

"What do you mean?" I asked.

Jack lowered his head. "You see, I wasn't really dancing. I was . . . well, to be truthful, I was imitating humans. I was making fun of the way humans move around. I thought the scissors people might like that, and they did."

Sam and I exchanged a surprised look.

"Smart of you," Curtis remarked. "Playing to their prejudices."

"Yeah, well, the scissors people had a funny way of showing their approval," Sam said. "Slamming into you like that."

"There's no gentleness in that crowd," Jack told us.

"Good thing we trained you how to keep your emotions in check," Sam pointed out.

"It was indeed," Jack replied. "My education was crucial to my success."

"What about giving them the virus? In your opinion, did they know what you were doing when you started touching blades with them?" Curtis asked.

Jack nodded, and his eyes opened wide. "Oh yes, they knew all right. They knew immediately. I think they could actually smell the virus. They're very clever in so many ways."

"But you succeeded," I told him.

"Barely. My mistake was, I went too slowly—they had time to react."

"Those three guys were pounding the heck out of you," Sam said.

"I thought they were going to kill you," Nim added.

"For a while, I did too," Jack said. "It was horrible pain. But somehow I managed to touch blades with each of them, and once I neutralized my attackers, I dug myself out of the sand. Then in the heat of the moment, I was able to fly faster than I ever imagined and touch every blade just before they had a chance to launch their attack."

"Bless your heroism," Mom said, leaning forward in a graceful bow, and we all followed her example.

84

"Now, Curtis, I have a question for *you*, if I may." Jack asked if any other humans—besides those in the room and Lex and, of course, David and Julie—were aware of their existence.

"Yes," Curtis admitted. Westfield's wife, the doctor, had learned of the activities of her husband and was trying to help the police find him. In the past few days she had finally realized the full extent of his villainy.

Earlier that day, when he reported David Westfield's activities to the authorities at MIT, Curtis had been forced to reveal the existence of both the scissors people and the card people. The president of MIT had decided that these developments were matters of national security, and she immediately informed the highest level of national government. The President now knew about the card people, and just hours ago, the joint chiefs of staff—the highest military leaders in the land—had been briefed on their existence.

"I wouldn't be surprised if this neighborhood is already full of CIA operatives and military officials—in fact, some of them may be lurking around outside even as we speak," Curtis said. "But I made them promise to give us a day or two of privacy before they start questioning us."

"What will happen then?" I asked.

"Well, as you can imagine, with anything that might compromise national security . . ." Curtis began.

"They're not taking the card people away," Sam declared.

I stood up, walked over to the window, and peered out into the darkness. All I could see was my own reflection, tired and anxious.

Curtis made a little face. "I'm afraid they can and they will, Sam. And it might be for the best. We're about to enter an exceedingly delicate and dangerous time."

"No one is taking the cards away!" I turned back toward Curtis and Mom.

"I'm with you!" Sam announced.

"Me too!" agreed Nim.

Mom stood up and walked over to me. She knelt down beside me and put her hand on my arm. "Paul, haven't we suffered enough already? I can't lose any more of our family. I just can't."

"The card people are family too, Mom."

"I'm sure wherever they go, they'll be well cared for."

"That's not the point." I crossed my arms. Sam scowled. Nim shook her head.

"Speaking as one of the card people, I'm sure we'll be glad to go wherever we can be of the most help," Jack offered. "We suspect that our mission is not over yet. And of course, with this crisis past, we fully intend now to begin the search for your father."

"No, Jack, he's—" Sam began.

"Why don't we talk about this later," Mom interrupted. "We've had a very long and difficult few days." A tear began to roll down her cheeks.

Nim jumped to her feet and put her arms around her. "I'm sorry, Mrs. Kapadia, I'm so sorry for all that you've gone through."

Mom was right. It had been a long and difficult few days, for everyone.

85

Nim was spending one more night at the house, and she was already settled in Sam's room when there was a little scratching at my door. Instinctively, I reached out and placed my hand on the box of cards under my pillow. They were safe.

"Who is it?" I asked.

Sam came into the room and sat down on my bed.

"I couldn't sleep," he said.

"I can't sleep either. What about Nim?" I asked.

"She's snoring."

I patted the cards again.

"I figured it out," Sam told me. He was trying to sound casual, but I could hear the excitement in his voice. He shifted his weight.

"Figured what out?"

"As a plum."

I sat up. "You figured it out?" I asked.

"Yeah. It was pretty easy, once you thought about it a little."

"What's it mean?"

"I'll show you." Sam grabbed a pad of paper and a pencil from my desk and sat down again on the bed. "Take a look at the letters."

In the pale orange glow of the nightlight he traced out:

A S A P L U M

"Now, rearrange those letters to make two names," he told me.

"OMG," I exclaimed softly.

I took the paper and pencil from Sam and wrote:

SAM   PAUL

"See how easy it was?" Sam asked. "But what's it mean?"

I shook my head. "He's not coming back," I murmured.

"What?"

"Dad. He's not coming back."

Sam shook his head. "What makes you think that?"

"Think of the question. 'How would you like to come back to life?' And how's he answer it?"

"With our names," Sam said.

"Right. It means that Dad knew the only way he can live on is through us," I whispered.

"I think it means he loves us," Sam contended, with a sad toss of his head.

"It means that too."

"Well, if he loves us, then he might come back."

I shook my head. "Sam, I don't think he's saying that. What he's saying is, we're all that's left."

"You don't know that for sure." He was silent for a minute. Then he spoke again, in a little voice that hardly sounded like his own, "Sometimes I get scared because I can't remember his face anymore."

"You still remember his face," I said fiercely.

"No, really, I lose it sometimes. I can't picture his face in my mind. Do you realize how horrible that is, Paul?" His body shook, and I handed him some tissues. He's usually a pretty happy kid, but when he cries, he goes all the way—big gooey sobs.

I put my arms around him.

I was beginning to realize that there were many levels to this. There was, in fact, a whole series of meanings, each inside the other, like one of those wooden puzzles where you open up one shape, only to find a smaller replica of the same shape inside it.

But in this case, the puzzle was as strange and as inside-out as nanotechnology itself, because each time you opened up one meaning, you found a larger—not a smaller—meaning inside.

Yes, it meant for starters that Dad would live on through Sam and me. And that contained a larger, sadder truth: Dad had accepted the fact that he would never be back in any other way. As Sam had intuited, that in turn meant that Dad loved us—he loved Sam and me—even more than he had loved his own life. Which meant that he trusted us to be as brave and as smart and as good as he had been.

And that led to one final conclusion: Sam and I had to help Dad finish his life's work.

We could never turn our backs on the card people and their mission.

By now, Sam had stopped crying and dried his tears.

"Go wake up Nim," I told him.

"Why?"

"She needs to text Lex. Tell her to have him fire up the Wagoneer and meet us at Children's Beach. We'll join them there in about half an hour."

"What are we doing?" Sam asked.

"They're not taking the card people from us. Not if I can help it."

"I'm with you," Sam whispered.

He stood up. He took one step toward his room, then stopped and turned back toward me. "Are you sure this is the right thing?"

"What other choice do we have?" I asked.

Sam nodded. "Okay. I'll wake her up." He started again toward the door, but he looked as if he might stop again at any moment.

"Bring a change of clothes," I called quietly after him.

"Right." Sam tiptoed out the door, and it closed quietly behind him.

86

I got up and stuffed a few things into my backpack—a change of shorts, a sweatshirt, a bottle of water. I found a granola bar and threw that in, for good measure.

That was all I had for now.

Was it enough?

I looked at the pitiful pile of stuff and shook my head. What had I been thinking?

Where would we go? What would we do to avoid being captured? How would we get enough food and money to survive?

For that matter, how could we even get more than five feet away from our house, with all the CIA agents out there?

And what would Mom's face look like when she woke up in the morning and we were gone?

Find your way to an answer, Dad had told us. But it was pretty clear that this wasn't it. And I knew that I had made some pretty serious mistakes in the past by making decisions too quickly, by not thinking through the consequences, like when we decided to trust David Westfield.

I sat down on the bed.

A minute later Sam was back in the room.

"I can't do it," he told me.

"I can't either," I said miserably.

Sam sat down beside me. "I didn't even wake up Nim."

"That's all right."

"We have to find some other way."

"I know." I cast my thoughts out into the night. "It's strange, but I think I can feel an idea coming."

"Can I sleep in here tonight?" Sam asked.

"Sure."

Sam dragged the mat out from under my bed, and I tossed down an extra blanket and pillow from my bed. Sam set up his bed, burrowed into it, and rolled around for a minute or two, trying to get comfortable.

"Good night, Paul. Sleep tight."

"Don't let 'em bite." That was what Dad had always told us at bedtime before he kissed us goodnight.

I climbed between my covers, reached under my pillow, and patted the cards one more time. I turned off the light. Against the velvet blackness of space, stars flickered like fireflies. Low in the southwest, Orion the Archer looked small and distant. It had already begun its journey to other realms.

I thought of Jack's strange journey—becoming a scissors person and venturing into a new and unknown world—and then, like a sparkle of sunlight on water, an idea flashed before my eyes. An idea that was far stranger and more daring than anything I'd ever thought of before . . . but I had a feeling it might just lead to an answer.

With the help of good friends, and some luck and good fortune.

I rolled over onto my side and closed my eyes, more at peace than I'd been in months. The vastness of the universe flowed over and around me like a living being, so close that I could feel its breath, its beauty, and yes, its silent splendor.

The End of Part I of The Card People *series*

ACKNOWLEDGMENTS

Thank you to my many readers, over several years, who helped me improve and refine this story.

To the fifth grade students of Nantucket New School who asked for a bedtime story on a camping trip, and a tale came to me about the card people and their cruel foes, the scissors people. To the students who later read the first draft of the novel and critiqued it.

To Julian and Talia Blatt (along with their parents Joe and Leda) who reviewed an early version and gave excellent advice about issues of pacing and clarity.

To Lalita Abhyankar, who offered invaluable feedback on some of the cultural issues surrounding the portrayal of an Indian American—including food!

To Caleb Kardell (a former student of mine and my wife Barbara's!) who created the fabulous artwork for the front cover.

To Ray Rhamey, for his exquisite book design.

To Karetta Hubbard and Molly Best Tinsley of FUZE, who helped me reshape the story and improve every corner of the novel.

ABOUT THE AUTHOR

James Sulzer, author of *The Card People,* lives on Nantucket Island, Massachusetts, where he taught students in grades 4 – 8 for close to thirty years. A graduate of Yale University, where he was a Yale National Scholar, he is also the author of *Nantucket Daybreak* (Walker and Co.) and *The Voice at the Door,* a novel of Emily Dickinson (FUZE Publishing). He has also produced countless "sonic id's" for National Public Radio.

This is his first published novel for children.

READERS GUIDE

General Questions:

Nanotechnology and new life forms:

1) This story describes some new forms of life that are kind and helpful to humans (the card people) and others that are scary and dangerous (the scissors people). In your opinion, should people try to create new forms of life? Why or why not?

2) What do you think of Jack and the card people? Would you like to know them?

3) After his first surgery, Jack complains:

> "What's the matter with all of you? You think this is some sort of freak show? Or are you just happy that I'm willing to risk my own life to save yours from the snappin' scissors . . . We card people sacrifice our lives again and again to save you. Does any human ever show any willingness to make a sacrifice?"

What do you think of Jack's statement? Does he make valid points? Why or why not?

4) If you had some "nanodust" that could make an inanimate object come to life, what would you choose to sprinkle it on? Why would you want that object to come to life?

Characters:

1) What has Paul learned about himself in the course of this story? What has he learned about the world around him?

2) How has Paul changed during the story?

3) How are the brothers Paul and Sam similar? How are they different?

4) How do Paul's feelings for Nim change in the course of the story?

5) Do you think Paul and Lex will be friends in the future? Why or why not?

6) A number of characters in this story need to learn how to control their anger or keep other emotions in check so they can make good decisions. What strategies can children or adults use to keep their emotions under control?

Extensions:

1) One theme of this book is that people who are seen as "different" can be of great value to others. The Kapadias are Indian Americans who seem different to Butch and Ken, and probably to some other neighbors in Bayview. Nim says she feels "different" because she is from Thailand, a country in Southeast Asia. Another hero in the novel is Curtis, who has Aspergers Syndrome, a form of autism. At first Paul and Sam are suspicious of Curtis because they think his behavior is strange, but later they accept him and feel a growing affection for him.

Write about someone you know who is "different" and is of great value to you and to others.

2) As he lies in bed at the end of the novel, Paul writes,

> I thought of Jack's strange journey—becoming a scissors person and venturing into a new and unknown world—and then, like a sparkle of sunlight on water, an idea flashed before my eyes. An idea that was far stranger and more daring than anything I'd ever thought of before . . . but I had a feeling it might just lead to an answer.

The reader can only guess . . . but what do you think is the "idea" that flashes before Paul's eyes?

3) Write a letter to the author, James Sulzer. Explain what you like about the book, and what you do not like. Do you have any suggestions to improve the book? Be sure to include examples to support your opinions.

STUDY GUIDE

Comprehension Questions—by section

PROLOGUE: *Dad's disappearance*

1) Describe the Kapadia family. What seems special about them? How are they unusual?

2) There are two "versions" about what happened to Dad. Which one do you believe? Why?

CHAPTER 1 – 6: *Meeting the Card People*

1) Describe the card people. How do they differ from one another? How do they behave?

2) What do you think Jack means when he says, "It's the same as the DNA in the teardrops that brought us to life"?

3) Describe the relationship of the two brothers, Paul and Sam. Use details from the reading to back up your ideas.

CHAPTER 7 – 9: *The Attack*

1) How do the card people avoid the attack of the scissors people?

2) How do the scissors people seem to communicate?

CHAPTER 10 – 11: *School*

1) What unusual occurrence does Paul see when he is walking to school?

2) How has Paul and Nim's relationship changed over the years?

3) Describe the bullies. Why do you think they are they picking on Paul? Does Paul fight back?

CHAPTER 12 – 15: *Back home*

1) What does Paul remember about his father while Nim is talking to Jack?

2) What do Paul, Nim, and Jack figure out about the tears that fell on the cards? What is Nim's concern about the tears?

3) Describe Paul's memories of his father.

CHAPTER 16 – 17: *Counterattack*

1) What is the card people's plan to disable the scissors people? Does it make sense to you? Why or why not?

2) What do Paul and Sam discover when they return home from the Haul-over? What action does Sam take? Do you think Sam made a wise decision. Why or why not?

CHAPTER 18 – 21: *School and Home*

1) What does Ms. Burns tell Paul? How does it affect Paul?

2) Is Paul starting to change in any way? If so, how?

3) What has Nim been making for the card people?

4) What does Nim tell Paul about how she has felt living in Bayview? What else does she reveal about herself and her feelings?

CHAPTER 22 – 23: *Mom's Accident*

1) What happens to Mom? How does Sam react? How does Paul react?

2) What is your opinion of Curtis? Do you think he is a friend to the boys? Why or why not?

CHAPTER 24 – 25: *Lex*

1) What new technology have the card people developed? What happens when they try it out?

2) How does Nim react when she sees Lex? What do you think she is feeling?

CHAPTER 26 – 29: *Mom Back Home*

1) How is Mom's health now? How can you tell?

2) What are the HOBO messages? What do you think they mean?

3) Describe the fight and the apology between the two brothers.

4) Who do Paul and Sam want to have a meeting with?

Why? How does Nim feel about this idea?

CHAPTER 30 – 33: *Westfield*

1) Describe David Westfield. Does Paul trust him? How can you tell?

2) Who is waiting for the boys and Nim when they leave the coffee shop? What does he tell them?

3) Back home, what does Sam do to try and have some fun?

CHAPTER 34 – 36: *School Attack*

1) Describe the remarkable events in math class that day.

2) Describe the guidance counselor, Mrs. Knockway. Do you think she understands what is really happening? Why or why not?

3) What do Paul and Nim do to make sure the scissors person is immobilized? What does Nim discover about Sam's boat?

CHAPTER 37 – 38: *More plans*

1) How is Brinda changing? Why do the children think she is changing?

2) What do Paul and Sam think of David Westfield now? What does Nim think of him?

3) On the next page is a passage from Chapter 38:

> Lex put his arm around Nim, and she rested
> her head on his shoulder. Something tumbled
> in my stomach like a wet load of laundry.

What is Paul feeling? What does this passage tell you about his feelings for Nim?

4) How have the card people immobilized the scissors people?

CHAPTER 39 – 40: *School Day*

1) What does Butch do when he sees Paul at the end of the school day? How does Paul feel about this encounter?

2) What does Paul see inside Curtis's car? What does Paul think it was used for, and why does this discovery seem important to Paul?

CHAPTER 41 – 43: *Second Meeting with Westfield*

1) In Chapter 41, what does Sam start to tell Westfield? Does Paul think that it is a good idea? How can you tell?

2) What does Westfield tell the boys about so-called "living creatures"?

3) What does Westfield do as he and the boys are leaving the coffee shop? How do the boys react?

CHAPTER 44 – 45: *Mom's Talk*

1) What does Mom tell the boys about their father's work? About Curtis? About David Westfield?

2) What information does Mom say she cannot tell them?

CHAPTER 46 – 47: *Driving to the Haul-Over*

1) What do Paul and Sam say to Curtis when they see him outside the house?

2) What does Paul realize when he sees Lex and Nim in the car together? How does he feel about it?

3) Is there anything wrong about Lex driving the car?

CHAPTER 48 – 52: *Rescue Attempt*

1) What is Paul and Sam's plan to rescue the cards?

2) What does Paul do to try and fool Westfield and Julie? Does his idea work? What does this plan show about Paul?

3) What role do Lex and Nim play in the attempted rescue?

CHAPTER 53 – 55: *Back Home Again*

1) How does Paul react to Curtis when he first sees him again?

2) What surprises Curtis about the card people?

3) What do Nim and Lex have a quarrel about?

4) Describe what happens when the card people try out their airplane.

CHAPTER 56 – 57: *New Plans*

1) Lex makes the suggestion that the military should *"blast that whole section of the Haul-over to oblivion."* According to Paul, why wouldn't this plan work?

2) What is Jack's plan to defeat the scissors people? What are the advantages of this plan?

3) Explain the "external restraints" that Curtis and Jack discuss. What is the purpose of these external restraints?

CHAPTER 58 – 61: *Surgery and its Effects*

1) How does Paul help Curtis unlock Jack's code? Where did the password come from?

2) Describe Jack's behavior after the surgery. How is it different from earlier? Include details to support your answer.

3) What was Curtis's mistake during the surgery? How does he plan to fix it?

4) Describe Jack's reaction to the Queen of Hearts.

5) At the end of one chapter Jack remarks, *"It's a very complicated thing to be a human, isn't it?"* What do you think Jack means when he says this?

CHAPTER 62 – 63: *Jack's Training*

1) What is the purpose of Jack's training? How do the children plan to accomplish it?

2) What does Sam say is wrong with the plan to disable the scissors people?

CHAPTER 64 – 65: *Getting Ready*

1) At the beach, Sam asks Paul, *"Has this whole thing—losing Dad, meeting the card people, fighting the scissors people—has it been good for you?"* Explain Paul's answer.

2) According to Jack, what is the purpose of the airplane?

CHAPTER 66 – 68: *More Changes for Jack*

1) Explain the changes in Jack after the new surgery. How well does Jack adapt to these changes?

2) Describe Paul and Lex's conversation in the kitchen. How does Paul feel, later, when he talks to Nim about that conversation?

3) What does Nim write at the bottom of the posterboard?

CHAPTER 69 – 71: *The Voyage*

1) *We said good-bye to Mom. "You'll be back soon?" she asked.*
"Yeah, Mom, soon," I told her. Her eyes lingered on me, but she said nothing more. She might have sensed that we had different meanings of the word soon.

What are Mom's and Paul's different meanings of the word *soon*? Why is this difference important?

2) As they are rowing across the bay, what do the children find in the water?

3) Describe the behavior of the scissors people on the lawn when the children first see them, and describe the shape they create.

CHAPTER 72 – 74: *Crisis*

1) What does Jack do when he is left out in the middle of the scissors people?

2) When Jack starts to float around the second circle, what happens to him?

3) What does Nim do when she sees Jack is in trouble? What does Paul then do?

4) Paul describes:

> As the grains of sand rained down on us, I said my good-byes to Mom, to Sam, to Dad, to the world.
>
> But what came next was not at all what I expected.
>
> I became aware of a vast chattering, an outburst of song, like the cries of countless birds; I heard the faint clank somewhere of metal on metal; I could swear I even heard a silver melody as pale and fragile as moonlight.
>
> Was this death?
>
> If so, it must be heaven, because it smelled like sunshine and roses.

What do you think is happening during this passage?

CHAPTER 75 – 76: *Afterwards on the Haul-Over*

1) What does Sam tell Paul about what happened?

2) What does Paul warn Jack not to do?

3) Describe what happens when Nim comes over to Paul. What is each of them feeling?

CHAPTER 77 – 79: *Back at Home*

1) What happens to Dad while he and Paul are playing cards?

2) What does Mom reveal to Paul about Dad?

CHAPTER 80 – 81: *Awake*

1) What are Paul and Sam worried that Westfield might do next?

2) Describe the meeting between Paul and Nim in Paul's room. What does Paul tell her?

CHAPTER 82 – 84: *Jack Becomes Himself Again*

1) Curtis asks for advice about whether or not he should put the external restraints back on Jack. What does he decide to do? Do you think this is a good idea or a bad idea? Why?

2) What does Jack reveal to the humans about his experience with the scissors people?

3) According to Curtis, what other humans are now aware of the card people?

4) According to Paul, who might try now to take away the card people?

CHAPTER 85 – 86: *Conclusion*

1) What does Sam finally figure out about his father's wish to come back to life "as a plum"? Had you figured this out already?

2) According to Paul, what was Dad trying to tell them with this secret message?

3) What do you think is Paul's "idea" at the end of the novel?

Pepperoni Palm Tree by Aidan Patrick Meath and Jason Killian Meath
A story about the only tree of its kind in the world and a boy named Frederick, this book portrays the challenge of being true to oneself and celebrates the uniqueness that enables each of us to shine, and thus enlighten the world. Children's Fiction.

Behind the Waterfall by Molly Best Tinsley
When identical twins Chet and Nash Eagleman and their younger sister Shyla move to a half-dead town in South Dakota, they stumble on an astonishing family secret that comes with special powers and a scary mission. They must take down the ruthless criminal who controls the town and aims to control the world. But how?

CPSIA information can be obtained
at www.ICGtesting.com
Printed in the USA
BVOW08s1600011116
466572BV00004BA/4/P